The Flannel Past

The Flannel Past

Matt Dahlgren

Also by Matt Dahlgren

Rumor In Town

This book is dedicated to Don Dahlgren, my dad and champion.

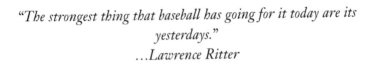

"The strongest thing that baseball has going for it today are its yesterdays."
…Lawrence Ritter

INTRODUCTION

~⁓

July 23, 2062

IT HAD BEEN A LONG time since he sat on the wrought iron bench that overlooked the lake. Fifty years to be exact, and nothing had changed. Not even the bench. The view was the same, the air was still clean and the promise of another day still loomed large. What had changed was him. He was older, wiser, and most of all content.

There was something magical about Otsego Lake. Its untellable spirit was evident from the moment David Danly gazed on its sparkling beauty so many summers ago. The lake, in the center of this tucked away town, was like a mirror that reflected greatness to the heavens. This was a place to lose concerns about the future and celebrate the past. The stores, restaurants, and small talk shared between perfect strangers evoked innocent reminders of yesterday.

Cooperstown, New York, is home to the Baseball Hall of Fame. The epicenter for lovers of baseball, and the place for storied legends to live in perpetuity. Aside from its palpable beauty, perhaps the most romantic aspect of it was the location. Far from city lights, sequestered from the clutter of humanity, this town was hidden; to get there took effort and a devotion for the national pastime.

For David, Cooperstown represented a beginning. It's where at the age of fifteen he became a man. It's where he learned to accept things out of his control and to control things that were unacceptable.

It's where he experienced the most magical two weeks of his life.

On this glorious day fifty years later, he looked across the lake as a subtle breeze blew through his thinning gray hair. He couldn't help but think about everyone who impacted his life. And then there were the others, the ones whose stories he kept near and dear to his heart, locked away.

Who would believe him anyway?

But he knew that somewhere in a place still unknown to even him they were all jubilant.

He reached into his coat pocket and removed a small, black leather Moleskine notebook. The old book was held together by a cracked, green rubber band. He peeled off the rubber band and removed an index card. In an instant his eyes swelled with tears. He read out loud, *"Because of you I found my voice. Use your passion and find yours."*

He smiled knowing this moment was perfect.

"Heaven on earth," he whispered.

CHAPTER 1

June 18, 2012

J IM D ANLY COULDN'T BELIEVE IT was 9:48. The glow from a blank Word document had remained that way for the better part of two hours. The screen was the only light inside the offices of the A. Bartlett Giamatti Research Center in the National Baseball Hall of Fame. An untouched Styrofoam box filled with mozzarella sticks from Nicoletta's Italian Café sat before him. The same could not be said for a bottle of wine from home. It was dry as dust.

In his younger days, Danly was a handsome man, but the years hadn't returned the favor. Though he liked to think his imposing blue eyes had withstood the test of time. His once golden hair thinned, was beginning to gray and he was two days past due for a shave. He stopped caring about his appearance long ago. Somewhere inside this sixty-four year old man was a shrewd business man who had made a lot of money in multi-million dollar land deals in Southern California. But that was another life. No amount of money could buy him happiness now.

An open folder containing black and white images of Earle Combs, the first in a long line of great Yankee center fielders, covered his desk. Combs was a teammate of Babe Ruth, which is how Jim justified looking at these timeworn photos instead of writing. It was research. Hours spent staring at old black and whites instead of writing was excusable. Procrastination was Jim's best friend; he'd find anything to do to avoid writing this book that had taken the better part of ten years.

It wasn't so much the story he wrote that clouded his thoughts, but his connection to it. After all, there were countless books on Babe Ruth. It seemed that every decade or so another biographer put their spin on the man who launched baseball, *sports* for that matter, into the monetary stratosphere.

Who needed another one?

When Danly would start to doubt the merits of his efforts, a book about the 1932 Yankees and Babe Ruth's infamous "called shot," he spent a moment looking at the aged baseball enclosed in the square case on his desk.

It was that ball that kept Jim up late at night.

He didn't know whether the story behind it, the one his mother told him over forty years ago, was legend or lore. She told him the ball that sat on his desk collecting dust was the one Babe Ruth hit out of Wrigley Field in 1932. Was it truth? Or an attempt to bend the truth to make a devastated young man feel something other than grief. He hated not knowing. And he hated even more the unsettling thoughts of mortality that arrested his emotions with regularity.

Charlie *"Knucks"* Danly was known in the old neighborhood as Mr. *Fix It*. His thick fingers were perpetually covered in grease, his knuckles scarred from years of hard labor. These knuckles got him his nickname. If he wasn't fixing something or treating the kids on the street to shaved ice, he listened to his beloved Cubs on a crackling transistor radio. Loving the Cubs was his job. Being a steamfitter on Chicago's north side was merely a place to forget about the their misfortunes.

Knucks was only forty-five when he died. He was working overtime on a Saturday when a violent explosion rocked the building. And just like that, at sixteen, Jim lost a father and best friend.

The day of the funeral fell on the first game of the 1964 World Series. It seemed that the entire neighborhood squeezed into the small Danly home to pay their respects. Jim withdrew from everyone. His mother realized how much he hurt. She pulled him away from the grieving friends and family to hand him a baseball wrapped in frail yellow tissue paper. She explained it was his father's most prized possession. He'd held onto it since he was thirteen years old. His father was thrilled the two of them had shared a father-son bond bridged by baseball, and he was about to give Jim the baseball himself. He looked forward to watching the upcoming series between the Cardinals and Yankees with Jim, but that would never happen.

Now, the death of his wife Catherine to cancer, and the tragic death of his son Bill, have forced him into exile where he's abandoned his family including his grandson for almost sixteen years.

Working at the Hall of Fame subjected Jim to many renowned collectors who all have their own account as to the whereabouts of the "called shot" ball. But how could that be unless his mother had lied to him all those years ago? Of course, it could be that his mother and father both believed it was the ball, but were wrong. He couldn't help but wonder why his father never mentioned the baseball to him. After years of listening to cynics, he doubted the ball's authenticity more than ever.

Another night raced to nowhere. He still needed to pick up food for his best friend, *Banks*, an aging golden retriever. He hadn't accomplished a damn thing, which was becoming the norm, and his confidence in finishing the book waned against life's proverbial clock ticking inside his head. He opened his bottom desk drawer and dropped the cork from his wine behind the last hanging file. There was a stash of corks to remind him of wasted nights. He turned off his computer, grabbed his keys and reached for the door when the phone rang.

Who could that be?

Without turning on a light he walked back to his desk and picked up the receiver. "Hello," he said almost in a whisper.

"Hi, Jim?" a soft voice on the other end of the line said.

Susie?

"I'm surprised you're still there. It's so late," she said.

"Is everything OK, Susie?"

"Everything's fine. It's good to hear your voice, Jim."

"It's good to hear yours, too. My God, it's been what, five...six years?" Jim asked.

"To be honest I've lost count," Susie replied. "I'm sorry to bother you so late, and I know its short notice, but I have a favor to ask of you."

Jim's silence was deafening.

"A favor?"

"The company I work for is based in London. I have to go for a week to attend a seminar and some other internal meetings. Then I have to go to New Orleans where my girlfriend is getting married. I'm her maid of honor."

"*Uh-huh.*"

"I was kind of hoping David could fly out and spend some time with you, Jim. I could have him stay at his friend's house but you know how fifteen-year-old boys can be if left alone. Besides, you haven't seen David in so long I thought it would be a good opportunity to get to know each other."

Jim froze with fear. The last time he actually saw his grandson was ten years ago when he was called to Southern California as a witness for the prosecution in a corrupt real estate scam. His time was limited, but he did manage to take Susie and David out to dinner in Newport Beach. Promises were made to stay in touch only to be broken by distance and time. To Jim, the next best thing was sending birthday or Christmas cards with crisp hundred dollar bills inside. And though it may have seemed petty, it gave him peace of mind that he was showing love for a grandson he didn't know.

The notion of spending time with David was terrifying. *What kind of Grandpa am I?*

His decision was made.

"I'd like that Susie. When do you want him to come?"

"I was hoping this Sunday!"

"On Sunday?" Jim asked surprised.

"I know. I'm so sorry-"

"Sunday, huh?" Jim repeated. "Yeah…yeah, that would be just fine, Susie."

"You're a life saver. I'll email you all of the flight information when I get it. Thank you so much, Jim. David really needs this."

Jim paused.

"So do I."

CHAPTER 2

THE CHIMES THAT HUNG FROM the door to Camilli's Steakhouse rattled when Arthur Page walked in. The restaurant was empty except for leftovers bellied-up to the bar in a separate room adjacent to the front door. An attractive young blonde with spiky hair and a sharp nose flipped through the reservations book. Glenn was busy behind the bar hanging wine glasses from the stemware rack. If it happened in Camilli's, Glenn had seen and heard it all. He'd been tending bar at his father's restaurant since he was a teenager. He was as sweet as puppy's breath and had shoulders wide enough to land a small airplane on. Throughout the years he forged relationships with some of baseball's greatest players who'd visit every summer for the induction ceremonies. His stories flowed like beer from a tap, and the town folks lined up just to hear them.

On this night, Camilli's was quiet.

Arthur took a seat on the far side of the bar, away from the dim overhead lights. He reached over the bar and helped himself to a few cocktail olives. He was fit for an older man. His pronounced jaw highlighted white teeth that seemed to ignite when he smiled. His slicked-back gray hair gave him the appearance of an aging Hollywood star, often causing passersby's to stop and wonder, but never comment.

He removed a pencil from his pocket and doodled on a small cocktail napkin as Glenn approached. "What'll it be tonight, Arthur?"

"Bourbon and water. Easy on the ice," Arthur replied.

Arthur reached over the bar again and grabbed a plastic drink sword and began poking his teeth with it. He surveyed the room and drew in a deep breath from his nostrils and let it out in the same fashion.

"Haven't seen you in a while, Arthur?"

Arthur smiled.

"Away on business again, huh," Glenn laughed. "You ever gonna tell me what you do?"

"Are you writing a book, kid?"

"Maybe."

"Well, leave out a page and make it a mystery."

Glenn laughed along with a couple of male patrons on the other side of the bar.

"How's business been for you?" Arthur asked.

Glenn removed a white towel from his waistband and rubbed a water spot on a wine glass. "It's been good.

Should pick up quite a bit next month for induction weekend!"

"I would imagine so."

"You gonna be around?"

"Oh, I doubt it. I'll probably get out of here to avoid all the crowds."

Glenn set a full glass on the bar. He kept his hand around it longer than usual, leaning to gaze into Arthur's hazel eyes hidden behind tinted reading glasses. "Seriously, where do you go all the time?"

"I get around," Arthur said, flashing his million dollar smile. "I'm like a leprechaun, kid."

The chimes on the front door rattled again as Jim Danly walked in. He took a seat on a stool at the center of the bar. Jim frequented Camilli's – usually for a nightcap before heading home. The news of David coming to visit hit him between the eyes; the excuse he needed to take the edge off.

Arthur watched with interest from his dark perch in the corner.

Glenn knew Jim's pleasure and poured him a glass of red wine. Jim grabbed the stem of the glass, and swirled it watching the wine roll around like the thoughts in his head.

"A penny for your thoughts, Jim," Glenn said.

Jim let out a deep breath. "Well, I was just hit with the news that my grandson is coming to visit."

Arthur removed his glasses and hung them from the collar of his shirt. He continued to doodle on the napkin, periodically looking up to study Jim.

"I didn't know you had a grandson," Glenn said.

"Yeah, I know."

"We've had a lot of conversations in here. I'm surprised you've never mentioned him. How long will he be here for?"

"A few weeks."

"When is he coming?"

"Sunday."

"You must be excited."

"I think I'm more nervous than anything," Jim said, staring into his wine.

"Hey kid, I'll take another one," Arthur said.

Jim turned and looked towards the dark corner of the bar. He hadn't noticed anyone over there. It took a moment for his eyes to adjust. When they did, he didn't recognize the older fellow.

"You'll have to bring him in so I can say hello," Glenn said.

"We'll see."

"Tell me…what's there to be nervous about?" Arthur chimed in.

Jim looked into the dark. "Did you say something?"

"Sorry, I heard you talking about your grandson."

Jim never talked about David and this conversation was becoming more awkward by the minute. "Let's just say I have a lot of catching up to do."

"That's OK. You've got time," Arthur said.

"I'm not so sure about that," Jim replied.

Glenn placed Arthur's drink in front of him and then filled Jim's wine glass. "So, what do you have planned for him?" Glenn asked.

"Hell, I just found out. I think I'm just going to play it by ear."

Arthur took a generous sip of his drink. He scrawled three words onto the napkin and folded it in half.

"What's his name?" Glenn asked.

"David," Jim replied.

"Does he like baseball?"

"I don't even know."

"Well, I'm sure you'll figure it all out."

"It's been years since I've even seen him. I don't even know what to give him."

Arthur downed the rest of his drink. "Give him a piece of yourself, and in return maybe he'll give you what *you* need." He pushed back from the bar and walked towards the front door. "Good night, fellas."

Jim stood and dropped a twenty on the bar. He was tired and still needed to get Banks' food. "It's been a long day, Glenn. I'll see you around."

"See ya, pal."

As Jim walked out the blond hostess stopped him. "Excuse me," she said. "The gentleman wanted you to have this." She held out a folded napkin. When he opened it his face felt flush.

Knucks says hello!

"What is this, some kind of sick joke?" Jim scoffed.

"I'm sorry. I don't know what you're talking about. He just gave it to me and left," she said.

Glenn overheard the commotion. "What's going on?"

"Glenn, who was that guy?" Jim asked.

"Who, *Arthur*? He's kind of a drifter. One day he's here, the next he's gone. I'm surprised you've never met him before."

"Where does he go?"

"Don't really know. But he always comes back."

"Well the next time you see him, call me. I'd like to talk to him."

"What's got you so riled up?" Glenn asked with concern.

Jim handed Glenn the napkin.

"Who's Knucks?" Glenn asked.

"My dad," Jim replied. "He's been dead for almost fifty years."

CHAPTER 3

~⁓

DAVID DANLY HADN'T LEFT HIS window seat the entire flight. He'd only flown once before. It was to visit his aunt in Seattle, and with his mother in tow. He didn't care much for flying, and cared even less for Seattle where it seemed to rain the entire visit. The thought of traveling across the country alone was daunting – but he'd never admit it.

He could think of a lot of places he'd rather spend his summer than the middle of New York. The only selling point was the home of the Baseball Hall of Fame. While David's knowledge of the history of baseball was limited, he loved to play the game and enjoyed watching it from time to time.

Bored from the flight, he found himself wondering about things, like the shy girl who sat in front of him in his creative writing class and on whom he had developed a heavy crush. *Would she look the same next fall? Would she even remember him three months from now?*

The struggles of adolescence were very real. Not having a father around to guide him through these turbulent times was proving to be significant. It was obvious to Susie as she was growing concerned with David's performance this past school year. Usually a straight-A student, David's grades dropped to Cs during his freshman year. And if that wasn't bad enough, he started hanging around a group of boys more interested in skipping class than learning something. David resented his mother for making him visit his grandfather. But she wasn't blind to the fact he was at an age where the influence of a man was needed. Her only other option was to have him stay with his friend Mike, but Mike spent the last two weeks of his freshman year suspended for drinking. While David wasn't with him at the time, and swears to his mom that he didn't do those kinds of things, Susie was reluctant to leave the two together without supervision. He had been a mama's boy – an absolute dream for any mother. But he was starting to test her with little things like not coming home on time, or doing his chores. Just little things, but Susie knew if left unchecked they could turn into bigger things. Time with his grandfather would do him some good.

~

What if I don't know what to say? What if he resents me? The anxiety built as Jim stared at the pages of the USA Today he bought outside the Syracuse Hancock International Airport. He folded the paper and tossed it into a trash can near the baggage claim as a wave of travelers appeared from an escalator. There were business men and women with cellphones stuck to their cheeks, mothers with nagging children, and elderly couples coming or going from visiting grandkids. At the end of the mass of people, walking alone, was an image from the past. If Jim hadn't been awake and aware of his surroundings he'd swear he was dreaming. From his striking green eyes and messy hair down to the way he swung his arms with each stride, he was a mirror image of Bill as a teenager.

David stared at the ground as he approached the baggage carousel. He didn't notice his grandfather only a few feet away. Jim watched, contemplating how he was going to make the awkward introduction, when, David turned and the two were eye-to-eye. The silence seemed to last forever. David paused. His grandpa seemed thinner than the last time and more gaunt in the face. Jim smiled and offered his hand. "Hi David," he said.

After a lengthy handshake, Jim pulled him in for a hug. "Come here, you," he said. "You look so much like your dad." The embrace lasted longer than David would have liked. When Jim finally let go, his eyes were watering. He tried to wipe them but David had already noticed.

"Sure is a long way from Southern California isn't it? How was the flight?" Jim asked.

David turned to grab his large black suitcase from the baggage carousel. "Not too bad."

"Are you hungry?"

"No. I'm good."

"Well let's get out of here then. We've got about a two hour drive ahead of us. Maybe we'll stop when we get a little closer to my house and grab an early dinner."

It was customary for Jim to find a shady spot to park his navy and tan Ford Bronco. New York summers could be brutal; with humidity so thick you could see it. They approached the car and Jim turned the key in the rear door to lower the back window. A golden snout with a touch of gray appeared. "Stay," he demanded. "Now you lie down and be a good boy."

"What's his name?" David asked.

"Banks."

"*Banks*?"

"Yeah, I named him after my idol growing up."

"Who's that?"

"So I see you're not much of a baseball fan! Ernie Banks...Mr. Cub...I grew up a big Cubs fan."

"My mom told me you were really into baseball."

"She did, huh?" Jim grabbed David's bag and winced when he threw it in the back of the truck. David noticed but didn't say anything. "What else did she tell you?"

Banks poked his head out the passenger window like he expected an introduction. "Hi Banks," David said while petting his shiny coat. "Do you always take him out with you?"

"Everywhere I go, he goes, unless I'm working," Jim replied. "Hey, you never answered my question."

"What question?"

"About your mom, what else did she say about me?"

"Nothing really, just to stay out of your way and not to bother you."

Jim smiled. "Banks get in the back. C'mon boy, let's go." Without missing a beat, he sprung to the back of the truck and curled up next to a pillow. "Hop in David."

They cruised along I-90 and the landscape flashed by like a movie in fast forward. David was struck by how green everything was, not like the gray images of big cities he'd conjured in his mind. Conversation was sparse, but Jim expected that. He didn't want to push things. It would take time to break down the barrier between them – a barrier he himself erected. Time was a precious commodity. He would make every attempt to amend his inexcusable absence.

Having David next to him in the car elicited flashbacks from rides he and Bill shared. Flashbacks like the two of them driving countless summer evenings along the Pacific Coast Highway enjoying the different views of the ocean, and the sun's glorious ways of saying goodnight. Jim and Bill were inseparable. The image of David brought him back to those moments that had somehow been lost but not forgotten.

"You sure you're not hungry? We're almost there. There's a neat little place up the road here called DiMaggio's."

David laughed. "Does everything in this town have something to do with baseball?"

Within a few minutes David acquiesced to his grandpa's dinner offer of chili dogs and cherry cokes where they continued the first steps of getting to know one another at a small table on the side of Highway 28.

The sun had dipped behind the Catskills by the time they drove into town. The streets were lined with old homes, mature trees, and no shortage of American flags that fell listless in the still night air. All so new and different.

They rolled towards the outskirts of town where the homes grew bigger, set further back from the street on generous plots of grass. They turned onto a long gravel driveway. David heard the rocks underneath the thick tires snap like hot popcorn. Jim pulled the car up to a large two-story white-washed home surrounded by large trees that punctured the night sky. David drew in a deep breath and slowly let it out. He missed California already.

CHAPTER 4

David couldn't escape the sun piercing through vertical blinds above his bed. He hadn't slept this well in a long time. After a full day of travel, the extra rest was welcomed. The house was quiet except for a group of birds outside conducting the most beautiful symphony. He pulled one of the blinds, mesmerized by the scene from his small upstairs window. A beautiful lake with speckled sunlight glistening across the surface appeared so close he believed he could reach out and touch it. When they arrived it was too dark to notice the landscape that hugged the back side of the house. Right outside his window were large sugar maple trees that looked like green cotton candy. An unencumbered patch of wild grass led to a splintered dock which extended into the calm water. He couldn't get out of bed fast enough.

Cooperstown didn't seem so bad after all.

The large grandfather clock in the corner of the living room ticked with precision like a metronome keeping life's beat. In the kitchen a note was propped-up between the salt and pepper shakers:

Had to go in early today! There's some fruit on the counter and cereal in the pantry. Help yourself to some coffee. On second thought, I don't even know if you drink the stuff. There's some juice in the fridge. I'll be back around noon. I'd like to take you to the Hall later to meet my co-workers…Grandpa.

This was his chance to inspect some things he'd noticed last night. There was a table in the living room with two framed pictures. One was a photo of a beautiful middle aged woman with soft brown eyes, a radiant smile, and perfect teeth. In front of the frame was a dried long-stem white rose with a gold wedding band around the stem. The other photo was a teenage boy. David could easily see it was his dad – the resemblance was uncanny. In front of that frame was a scuffed baseball with the words *Bill's first home run* written across the sweet spot. He had never seen a picture of his father as a boy.

A small library was off the living room. It had a large bay window with an amazing view of the lake. A leather Barcalounger with tuft-back upholstery was next to the rock fireplace. A pad of paper and pen rested on a small glass table next to it with bits of pistachio shells scattered about. The walls were lined with custom cherry-wood bookshelves from floor to ceiling. He took a moment and studied the titles. He was amazed his grandpa could have read so many books. There were presidential biographies and books on U.S. history, but the overwhelming majority of the titles were on baseball.

He approached the shelf and removed a book titled *October 1964*. He read the inscription on the title page written in blue ink.

> *Dad, I know how much the '64 season meant to you and grandpa. I can only hope to have a son to share the game with the way you have with me. We'll find out soon, huh? Happy Father's Day! Love, Bill (6/16/96).*

David read it three times before he grasped the impact of the message. He was born two months after his father penned those wishful words. And two months after that he was gone. His heart felt like it was going to leap out of his chest. He closed the book and put it back. David had no idea of the bond the game of baseball wove between his father and grandfather. Why would he? He didn't know either man. But as he stood there shocked, whatever contempt he harbored towards his Grandpa began to melt away. It began to make sense why his grandpa was so obsessed with baseball, and why he moved to Cooperstown. It was the only thing keeping him close to his son.

He got dressed and stuffed his backpack with a bottle of water and some cookies he'd found in the pantry. Banks was lying in the doorway to the library with the saddest looking brown eyes he'd ever seen. Banks was nobody's fool – this was all a ploy to get David to take him – and it worked. He grabbed the retractable leash next to the door and fastened it to Banks' collar and off they ran, letting the door slam.

A thick fog began to roll over the far side of Otsego Lake, and with it an unusual chill for a June morning in Cooperstown. David went for the trail behind the house. It stretched along the edge of the lake exposing the picturesque setting. He was surrounded by large trees that cast a perpetual coat of shade, leaving the smell of damp dirt in the air. For the most part, Banks was well behaved. But there were a few times he went splashing into the water – leash and all – trying to chase after a stone David had thrown.

This was all new to David. He'd never been camping, or spent any time in the outdoors, and the tranquility of it all: the rolling green hills, clean air, and birds high above seemed adventurous when adventure was what he needed. Walking the trail with Banks made him feel like a character in a Mark Twain novel – and he liked it.

Banks was a compliant partner along the way, but somehow he managed to get his back legs tangled in the leash. David decided to remove the leash all together. They continued around the bend where a long narrow point protruded into the water. On the edge of the point was a shade tree with a bench beneath it. An elderly man sat alone, giving David pause.

From where he stood the bench was about a hundred feet away; close enough for the gentleman wearing a green cashmere sweater and camel newsboy hat to hear the commotion between David and Banks as they rounded the corner. The older fellow turned and waved, almost enthusiastically. He had an odd smile as if he recognized David.

"Hi kid," the man said in a raised voice.

"Hi," David replied.

"You must be Jim Danly's grandboy?"

Not sure whether to answer, David nodded his approval while trying to get a better look at the guy. But between the shadows from the tree hanging over the man's head and the dense fog approaching the shoreline, it was difficult to see him. His large sunglasses didn't help. "Who are you?" David asked.

"Me? Oh I've been around these parts for a long time. I come and go," he said while rolling a newspaper with his thick hands. He started to walk around the bench, taking a step towards David. "I'm like a leprechaun, kid."

That moment, Banks took off running in the opposite direction after something in the bushes. David panicked. "Banks!" he yelled. He started after him. "Get back here Banks!"

Banks knew better than to exert too much energy chasing a foolish rabbit and decided to pull up before the sprint became a marathon. When David caught up to him he attached the leash to his collar and turned back towards the bench.

The old man was gone.

CHAPTER 5

JIM AND DAVID WALKED ALONG the crowded sidewalk towards the museum. Main Street was alive with fans carrying souvenirs, going from store to store, to indulge in their favorite pastime. Banners hung from street lights, and posters lined store fronts, featuring future inductees: Barry Larkin and Ron Santo. Induction weekend was a month away, but the town was already ramped up and excited with anticipation. Cars moved like molasses down the two-lane road making parking nearly impossible, which is why they decided to walk. "I'm afraid I don't know any leprechauns," Jim said. "What did he look like?"

"I couldn't tell. It was hard to get a good look at him. Banks took off in the other direction and when I finally caught up to him, I turned around and the guy was gone," David explained. "He had kind of a Boston accent if that helps any?"

"Not really. To be honest, I don't know too many people here in town."

"But you've lived here fifteen years!"

"I keep to myself, David. I like it that way."

All talks of leprechauns came to a halt when David's attention averted to the beautiful two-story red brick building across the street. The building was clean and evoked a sense of innocence like it popped out of a Norman Rockwell painting. On the ground level leading to the main entrance were three identical archways with double gold framed glass doors in each arch. Above the doors etched in a traditional gold font it read: NATIONAL BASEBALL HALL OF FAME AND MVSEVM. American flags hung from the outside walls. Below them were large ceramic flower pots with bright red tulips standing at attention.

"We're supposed to meet Martha Gallagher when we get inside," Jim said.

"Who's she?"

"She's the director of collections."

"Sounds pretty important."

"It is," Jim replied as he held one of the glass doors open. "She practically runs the place. I have a meeting that's going to chew up about an hour. I thought maybe Martha could show you around."

The main entrance was full of diehards reading maps and pamphlets about the Hall's various exhibits. Everywhere you looked were pictures of Barry Larkin and Ron Santo.

The museum had only been open for an hour yet the souvenir store inside was already thriving. "C'mon, follow me," Jim said.

They broke away from the commotion and entered a long corridor just around the corner. It was a gallery of greatness. If there was a cathedral for baseball, this was it. Black marble pillars and granite floors encased wooden walls where shiny copper plaques hung beneath the year of their induction.

David was in awe. "This is amazing."

"Isn't it?" Jim replied. "C'mon, I want to show you something."

The high ceilings and large windows allowed natural light to shine down giving the open corridor a sanctuary-like feeling. The gallery was full of people, young and old, who traveled from all over the country to take pictures next to the plaques of their childhood heroes. There were grandfathers and fathers with tears in their eyes explaining various players' greatness from summers gone to their sons and daughters. It was an extraordinary shrine, and David was hooked. He wanted to read every word on every plaque.

At the end of the long room were the founders of this great sanctuary – a wall that read '1936: The First Class'. "You see these guys, David?" Jim said pointing to the wall. "Without them, this place wouldn't be here." David stared at the wall and read the names: Christy Mathewson, George Herman Babe Ruth, Tyrus Raymond Cobb, Honus

Wagner and Walter Perry Johnson. "These five guys were the first to be inducted into the Hall of Fame and I bet you've only heard of Babe Ruth, huh?"

"I've heard of Ty Cobb," David fired back.

"It's a shame kids your age don't know more about the history of the game. But I bet you could tell me all the players who have shamed it by using performance enhancing drugs. *These* are the guys who planted the seeds, and plowed the fields, to harvest the game into what it is today. You oughta make it a point to learn more about them while you're here."

"So this must be David," said a woman who approached from behind. The two turned and were greeted by Martha Gallagher who carried a baseball cap with the Hall of Fame logo on it. She was middle-aged with short red hair and freckles, and she looked like she'd never been in a foul mood a day in her life. The only girl in a staunch Irish Catholic family full of boys from Boston's North End, Martha's father would routinely take her to Fenway Park. And if they weren't praying in the pews of St. Stephen's Church, they put their faith in the hands of Ted Williams and Carl Yastrzemski.

Jim and Martha had become close over the years in a brother-sister kind of way. They had a running joke between them about whose team would win the World Series first: Red Sox or the Cubs. The record would show that the last decade was kind to Martha and predictably dubious for Jim.

"David, I want you to meet Martha Gallagher," Jim said.

"Hello Mrs. Gallagher," David said.

"Oh, what manners. Please, call me Martha," she said with a smile. "I understand your grandpa would like me to give you a tour?"

"Sure, I'd love that."

"David, if you follow Martha around you'll know more about these five guys on the wall than any book could ever teach you."

Martha blushed. "I don't know about that Jim, but I'll do my best."

"I'll catch up with you guys after my meeting."

Martha smiled and put the baseball cap on David's head. "Don't worry about us Grandpa. Take your time."

He smiled and walked away. *Grandpa* had a nice ring to it, he thought.

"Is there anything you'd like to see in particular?" Martha asked.

David adjusted his new hat. "It's all so incredible. I'd kind of like to see some old uniforms. Are there any on display?"

"Of course! They're upstairs. C'mon."

The research center was closed for its monthly meeting so staff could catalogue all of the new arrivals donated to the

Hall. Every now and then family members of players or old fans who've passed away would donate their collections of photos and scrapbooks. On occasion, bigger items like bats, gloves and uniforms would arrive on the doorstep usually causing the employees to gather around like giddy children on Christmas morning. More times than not, these meetings amounted to nothing more than rehashing old baseball stories.

Michael Witz was a twenty-one year old self-avowed baseball expert. His father, Larry, was a high-profile New York City attorney whose handsome annual donations to the Hall provided great job security for Michael, recently graduated from Syracuse University. He spent the better part of his college years collecting and trading baseball memorabilia making him an expert in the field – all you had to do was ask. Some of the longer standing members of the library staff found Michael as irritating as a rash. They learned early to brush him off due to his know-it-all approach in dealing with pretty much everything.

The topic floating around the room on this day was whether or not Babe Ruth would be a formidable home run hitter in today's game.

"There's no way Ruth could hang with the pitchers of today," Michael said.

Stan Mills, the Director of Research, looked over his wire-rimmed glasses and responded with a touch of sarcasm. "Yeah, you're right Michael. No way!"

"C'mon Stan, you really think Ruth would dominate today?"

"Sure do."

"Please. I understand *Jim's* infatuation with Ruth, but…"

"Excuse me?" Jim interrupted. "*My* infatuation with Ruth?"

"We all know you're hung up on that ball you have. But I hate to tell you, it's not real," Michael quipped.

"Leave it alone, Michael," Stan said.

"Michael do you know how many people have told me that over the years?" Jim asked. "How many people claim to know the whereabouts of that ball?"

Michael couldn't look at Jim, "I'm sure a lot. But I know the guy who has it."

"Oh, you do?"

"Yeah, he's out of Denver."

"Damn it, Michael, drop it," Stan insisted.

"Denver, huh?" Jim asked.

Stan didn't like where this was going. He and Martha were the only two people who understood Jim's sensitivities towards that baseball. He had seen this before, and it usually resulted with Jim angry.

"All right…all right. Michael, I'd like you to go down to the vault and make sure all the carts are in order. Thank you." Stan said.

The door to the research center opened and David and Martha walked in. David was thrilled by the tour Martha had given him, but Jim's sour mood quickly put a damper on things. Martha surveyed the landscape and could tell tensions were high. She too was acutely aware of Michael's ability to agitate.

"How's everything going?" Martha asked with a touch of sarcasm.

Stan flashed Martha a look as if not to ask. Michael exited through a door in the back of the room with a large sign overhead that said STAFF ONLY.

"I sent him down to the vault to make sure everything was in order," Stan explained. Martha nodded.

"Vault?" David asked.

Martha smiled and tugged on the bill of his new hat. "It's a climate controlled room where we keep all of the belongings that aren't on exhibit."

"Like more jerseys and stuff?"

Martha laughed. "Yes, like more jerseys and stuff. It's off limits to the general public. Maybe one of these days we'll go down there and I'll show it to you. What's with you and these jerseys anyway?"

"I don't know. I just love the way they look. They're like pieces of art," David replied.

Jim walked into his office and closed the door without even acknowledging Martha and David.

"Stan, what just happened?" Martha asked under her breath.

"He and Michael had a little spat over the baseball." Stan removed his glasses and cleaned them with the bottom of his shirt. "You know how he gets."

"Looks like more than just a spat," Martha said.

"What baseball?" David asked.

Stan turned to David, "Oh, I'm sorry, you must be Jim's grandson? I'm Stan."

David extended his hand, "Hi."

Stan and Martha weren't going to be the ones to explain it to him. "Martha, I just received confirmation that the Boy Scout troop from Albany will be here tomorrow for their tour. I'll have Michael bring some things up from the vault and we'll put together a little display for them."

"Oh great, I'm so glad to hear they decided to come."

David excused himself and walked to his grandpa's office. He looked through a narrow window and saw Jim inside holding a small square case with a baseball inside. He could see the consternation in his grandpa's eyes. It was obvious he was upset, but he didn't know why.

CHAPTER 6

THE PIZZA PARLOR WAS OFF Main Street a couple of blocks from the Hall of Fame. The front of the restaurant had large open-aired windows that allowed the ambiance of the street to spill inside. Jim and David had a small table by a window. The warm night air and constant street chatter acted as a buffer between the awkward periods of silence. The walls inside were full of baseball pennants, posters, old hats and dusty gloves from some of the town's little league legends. Near the front door there were photos of Hall of Famers from over the years enjoying a slice of pizza with Vic, the proud owner. It was always easy to spot the locals too; they were the ones without bags of souvenirs on the floor.

A teenage girl placed a large pepperoni pizza in front of Jim and David and walked away. Jim took a sip of beer from a frosty mug and grabbed a slice. "Go on, help yourself." David grabbed a slice and watched a long strand of cheese stretch out before him.

"Martha seems like a neat lady," David said in an attempt to break the ice.

"She's the best. A real sweetheart!"

"You don't care too much for that guy, Michael, do you?"

"Why do you say that?"

"I can just tell."

"He's got a lot to learn."

"What about…the baseball?"

Jim pretended not to hear the question and chugged the remainder of his beer. He pushed back from the table.

"Be right back. You want another Coke?"

"Sure."

Jim returned with two cold mugs. "So you're going to be a sophomore, yeah?"

"Yeah," David replied between bites.

"That's great. So I bet you're wondering what in God's green acres you're doing here, aren't you?"

"No. It's all good."

Jim smiled. "All good, huh?"

Across the street on a busy corner was a coffee shop with circular umbrella tables out front. Arthur took a seat at one of the tables and positioned himself behind a curbside tree. A steady stream of foot traffic passed giving him just the interference he needed. He squeezed a packet of honey into his hot tea and stirred it gently, never taking his eyes off of Jim and David. From his perspective they seemed to enjoy the night, though the conversation appeared contrived. He knew the value of *time*, and how important it was not to waste it. If his plan was going to work he needed to act fast.

~

It was after ten o'clock and the museum was closed. Jim explained to David he had some things he needed to work on, and as long as he was by the front door at eleven he didn't care what he did. This was the opportunity David wanted; to go back and view some of the exhibits he'd seen earlier in more detail.

He left the research center and made his way down a curved ramp where famous documents hung on display. At the base of the ramp was the plaque gallery. This was his chance to finally read them. But where would he begin? *The First Class*, he thought. After all, they were the ones his grandpa told him were so important.

He reached up and rubbed his hand over the copper face of Babe Ruth as if he was reading braille. He did the same to Cobb and Johnson, but Mathewson and Wagner were out of reach. He read the brief biographies for each one, took a few steps back, and stared at the wall. It was so quiet, almost eerie. He turned and began to walk through the long gallery. When he got to the end, he veered to his right and walked up a small ramp called Inductee Row. Here were display cases featuring belongings to the newly inducted Santo and Larkin. From there, he went up a staircase to the second floor where the layout was like a maze of various snap shots leading from one room to the next, giving a detailed glimpse into the history of the game. Exhibits along the way included: 'Taking the Field: The Nineteenth Century', 'The Game: 1900-1930', 'Babe Ruth Gallery', 'Pride and Passion', and 'The Game: 1930-1970' were all exhibits along the way. Everything from jerseys, hats, gloves, bats, and personal mementos from watches to awards filled glass cases for all to see. David stopped to look at a Christy Mathewson jersey worn by the big right-hander during a world tour in 1913. It was gray with charcoal-colored pinstripes, and had an unfurled American flag patch on the left sleeve. NEW YORK was sewn across the front in faded red, almost pink, flannel letters. A gold pocket watch was next to the jersey as well as an old beat-up five-fingered glove. There was a set of red and white checkers in their original box that once belonged to Mathewson, and a brief description claiming he once beat world checkers champion, Newell Banks.

He continued through the exhibits stopping at Lou Gehrig's locker – somehow he missed that on his tour with Martha. He admired the simple beauty of the gray jersey with navy block letters across the front. A red, white, and blue patch on the left sleeve commemorated baseball's hundredth year and added a little color to the unpretentious garment. This was Gehrig's last jersey; the one he presumably wore in 1939 on the day he removed himself from the lineup after 2,130 consecutive games. On the top shelf of the locker was a hat worn by the Yankee captain, and a trophy given to him by his teammates, on that indelible July day when he stood before a packed house in Yankee Stadium declaring himself the luckiest man on the face of the earth.

The exhibit came to an end at a black partition. Behind it were restrooms and an elevator that had a STAFF ONLY sign. He turned to head back when he heard a faint rumbling from below. It was the elevator, and it grew louder by the second. He stood motionless waiting to see who would step off. When the doors opened, the elevator was empty.

He had assumed it was his grandpa.

He retraced his steps back through the second floor, unable to stop being creeped out by the elevator. For unexplainable reasons, he turned and began to walk back. The walk turned to a jog; the glass exhibits became a blur. He hoped the doors to the elevator would be closed and the notion of exploring parts closed to most would be put to rest. But the doors were wide open and inviting for a teenager with excess curiosity running through his veins, permission to go anywhere, and time to kill.

He stepped inside with caution – like a kid sneaking in after curfew.

The elevator descended at a slow pace. His heart started to race, his mind not far behind. He had to concoct an alibi.

What if somebody was there when the doors opened? What would he say? He would tell them that he got lost while looking for his grandpa. It was the only thing that sounded reasonable.

It came to a stop. After a lengthy pause, the doors opened. David stepped out, but remained still trying to listen for any other sign of life. He knew he shouldn't be there. But the thrill running through him was too strong; nothing could convince him to turn back. He was flanked by long hallways with white cinderblock walls, and shiny cement floors that seemed to stretch without end.

He walked the long hall to the left, and noticed what appeared to be a credit card on the ground. He picked it up. It was solid plastic with a numerical code at the bottom. There was a large metal door a few feet away. Next to the door handle was a black security pad. He figured the card was a key to open the door. A familiar sense eased over him, almost like he'd been here before. It was as if the open elevator and the access card were crumbs leading him into a leap of faith. Although he didn't know where he was going, something inside his soul called for him to find out. He looked down the long hallway to make sure no one was coming. Once he knew the coast was clear, he waved the card in front of the security pad. The door made a loud clicking sound. He pulled on the metal handle and it opened. There was an immediate drop in temperature and a wave of cool air rushed toward him carrying the smell of cleanliness that filled his nostrils. *This must be the climate controlled vault*, he thought.

The room was well lit and exceptionally clean. Along the left side were long rectangular boxes, hundreds of them neatly stacked on top of one another on shelving that ran the full length of the room. To his right were floor to ceiling metal doors with three pronged spindle wheel handles that opened up to additional storage areas. The collection of memorabilia was overwhelming. He began to walk the center of the narrow room. About half-way down he spotted a box to his left. The name MATHEWSON was written in black ink on the lower left corner. Then he noticed all the boxes had names written on them. He stared at the box for several seconds, deliberating on whether or not to remove it or leave the vault all together. He took the box down and placed it on a table in front of him and removed the lid.

Nestled in tissue paper like fragile eggs in a nest was an off-white flannel jersey folded in half. Its long sleeves were creased perfectly at the shoulders and laid flat over the front of the garment. It had thick black pinstripes with an interlocking NY on the left arm. It was a thing of beauty. David began to rub the lower portion of the shirt between his fingertips. He couldn't believe that he was actually touching it.

Taking the jersey out of the box was the wrong thing to do. Perhaps if Martha was there she'd do it for him. But she wasn't there, and he didn't know whether this chance would ever present itself again. He removed the jersey from the box with the hands of a surgeon and unbuttoned the front slipping his skinny arms inside.

He began to feel lightheaded and his vision blurred. The blurred vision turned to a feeling of faintness while muffled sounds of crowds cheering and umpires barking balls and strikes filled his head. The sensation of going in and out of consciousness grew strong; as did the melodic sounds of an old train clattering along aged tracks when everything went *BLACK.*

THE CHRISTIAN GENTLEMAN

The constant rocking motion of the Pullman car along with plumes of cigarette smoke woke David from his slumber. His head rested against a cold window of blackness, darkened by the Midwestern night. From his vantage point the car was empty but for the fellow who had fallen asleep hours prior due to generous portions of whiskey, and a group of four men up front engaged in a rousing game of cards. Their occasional roars of intoxicated laughter would cause the lone drunkard to stir in his seat only to shift and begin snoring again within seconds.

David remained still with his eyes half open. He pretended to be asleep while trying to figure out where he was and why he was wearing wool knickers, a tweed sport coat, and stiff leather boots that ran well up over his ankles.

Is this a dream?

He stood and made his way out to the aisle while at the same time being mindful of the vociferous group up front. The last thing he wanted was for them to see him and have this dream come to an abrupt end. He glanced to the back of the car. It was abandoned with the exception of a young man tucked away in a booth. He held a copy of Victor Hugo's *Toilers of the Sea* to his face. The glow of a lone candle exposed his indisputable good looks. His hair was neatly combed and his dark-gray suit looked like it had just come off the rack in one of New York's finest haberdasheries. There was something reassuring about him; a gentleness that comforted David.

He began to walk down the aisle towards the man. When he got within a few steps the fellow put down his book and smiled. "You've been out for quite some time," he said. "The boys up there have been making a lot of ruckus. Pretty much cleared out the whole car."

"Was I asleep?" David asked.

"Yes."

"For how long?"

"About an hour, I suppose," he answered. The man wedged a bookmarker between the pages and placed it on the freshly varnished table in front of him.

"What time is it?" David asked.

The man removed his pocket watch from his coat pocket. It looked exactly like the time piece David had seen in the Christy Mathewson exhibit.

"Half past eleven."

"Where am I?"

The fellow looked out his window into the darkness, "Somewhere between St. Louis and Pittsburgh!"

David expected his Grandpa to barge through the door any minute telling him he needed to come home.

Home?

Where is home?

Where am I?

The train hit a rough patch and began to sway causing David to lose his balance. "Why don't you move some of my things over and have a seat," the man said?

David grabbed the brown leather bag from the bench and handed it over to the man who leaned and set it in the aisle. David lifted a folded newspaper and set it on the table exposing a box of red and white checkers.

Gold pocket watch?

Checkers set?

He took a seat and held the box of checkers. He examined the pieces while the man looked on. "You play?" he asked.

David shook his head no and swallowed hard. "What's your name?"

"Christy."

"Christy Mathewson?"

He smiled, "That's right."

David looked to the front of the train. The raucous group of guys began to clear out. The lone drunk was still asleep. David looked back at Christy who looked out the window.

"Is this a dream?" David asked.

Christy ignored the question and continued to stare out the window into the darkness. Next to Mathewson was a journal. The pages were dog-eared, full of handwritten notes and stuffed with newspaper clippings.

"What's that?" David asked pointing to the leather bound book.

"Just some writing I'm working on."

"Writing?"

Christy folded the journal shut, "Mmhmm."

"What are you writing?"

Christy looked at David and smiled. "You're an inquisitive young man, aren't ya?" He grabbed his journal and stuffed it into his leather bag. "I'm working on a children's book."

"I didn't know you were a writer," David said.

"Why would you?" Christy asked perplexed. "I haven't written anything yet."

"Mr. Mathewson, how come…."

"Please, call me Christy."

"OK. Can I ask you something, Christy?"

"Go right ahead."

"How come you weren't up there playing cards with the guys?"

Christy paused and looked over David's shoulder. "You can spend your day's playing cards with the boys, but I'd rather spend my time reading and writing. There's much more to life than baseball and getting drunk with the fellas. Besides, baseball's a thinking man's game, especially for a pitcher. I have to be one step ahead, sometimes two steps. That's why I read a lot…to stimulate my mind, it keeps me thinking. Baseball's not forever you know! You better learn how to use what's between your ears, if you know what I'm saying."

David couldn't help but think about the times he'd skip class and sit behind the football stadium back home. He thought about all the times he clashed with his mother, often resulting with her in tears.

Christy reached into his coat pocket and removed a small leather Moleskine notebook. He took the cap off of his fountain pen and signed his name inside the front cover. "You've got a gift and you don't even know it. Here…I want you to have this." He handed the small book to David. "It's brand new. I carry one with me all the time."

"What is it?"

"A notebook."

David opened the inside front cover and inspected the freshly signed name, rubbing his fingers over the top of it.

"You should carry it with you wherever you go," Christy said. "You never know when you're going to see or hear something you want to remember. Besides, with all the questions you ask, you're bound to get some notable responses. Who knows, it could be the key to your future."

David glanced at the dateline on the *St. Louis Post-Dispatch* in front of Christy. August 1, 1911. The train sped along for several minutes where not a word was uttered between the two. Christy sat comfortably rocking back and forth to the train's rhythm. David just stared out the window until Mathewson broke the silence.

"Are you hungry? I can have 'em whip something up for you."

"I'm OK," David replied.

"So what are you thinking about?"

"I'm not sure."

A door to the adjoining car opened behind Christy. A porter entered wearing a gray coat with silver buttons lining the front. He had a high collared white shirt and thin black bow tie. He stood in the aisle next to Mathewson and removed his porter's hat. "Hi Matty," he said.

"Hi boss," Christy replied.

"I've got your bed turned down. You should probably hit the hay, huh? Those Pirates are gonna be raring to go tomorrow."

The porter's voice had a distinct sound to it. David had heard it somewhere before. He shifted in his seat to look up just as Christy blew out the candle, making the back of the train virtually dark. The man in the aisle took a couple of steps toward David and placed his hand on his shoulder. David glanced over to Christy who smiled at the porter.

"You said I have a gift earlier. What is it?" David asked.

Christy watched a blue stream of smoke from the candle drift upwards.

"It's called curiosity," Christy said.
"I think it's time to go now, kid," the porter said.
And then everything went black.

CHAPTER 7

DAVID HARDLY SPOKE A WORD on the short drive home. He turned down Jim's offer to watch television together and went straight to his room. On his bed, he and replayed the entire night over and over again; the vault, the jersey, Christy Mathewson, and the recognizable voice of the porter. After two hours of staring at the ceiling, he went downstairs to Jim's study. He scoured the bookshelves until he found what he knew his grandpa would have – a biography on Christy Mathewson. He removed it from the bookshelf and sat in the Barcalounger where he began to pour through it looking for clues or traits about Mathewson. He stayed up reading well into the early hours of the morning. The last time he remembered hearing the chimes of the grandfather clock in the living room was at four o'clock.

The smell of bacon was more reliable than any alarm clock could ever be. David opened his eyes to be greeted by Banks, whose moist snout was inches away. The sound of grease popping around the corner was all he needed to hear. He'd spent the entire night trying to process what had happened, and none of it made any sense. He wondered if it even happened at all, or if it was the most realistic dream he'd ever had. Maybe he had fallen asleep inside the vault and drifted into a secret world of sorts. After all, it was late and he still hadn't adjusted to the time change.

Banks began to nudge David's ribcage prodding him towards the kitchen. "OK, OK," he said. He pulled himself from the chair, Banks followed close behind.

His eyes were half open, hair unkempt, and he wore the same blue jeans and T-shirt from the day before. He sat at the table without acknowledging Jim, who stood over the stove putting finishing touches on breakfast. There was a copy of the *Cooperstown Crier* next to a glass of orange juice on the table. Jim held his gaze on David in an attempt to start a conversation, but David didn't notice; he just flipped through the paper staring mindlessly at the pages. A small television next to the table played the day's news in black and white, but neither of them listened.

"Is everything OK?" Jim asked. "You didn't have a whole lot to say last night on our way home." He set a plate in front of David.

"Everything's fine," David assured him.

"Anything you want to talk about?"

David didn't answer. He just shook his head and shoved a piece of bacon into his mouth. Jim knew that something was on his mind. Perhaps he was homesick. But he also knew that trying to pry things out of a teenage boy was like taking a bone from a dog. After several minutes of silence, Jim stood from the table and scraped the remaining eggs from the frying pan into Banks' bowl. Banks jumped from beneath the table and dashed to scarf them down.

"You sure there's nothing going on?" Jim asked. "Did something happen?"

David pushed the newspaper aside. "No. Nothing."

Jim finished drying the pans and wiped the counter clean. "Well then...I need to run. I've got a busy day today. You're more than welcome to stop by the museum today and walk around if you'd like."

"I think I'll just hang around here."

"Suit yourself. I've got some steaks in the refrigerator. I'll throw them on the barbeque when I get home this evening. Sound good?"

"Sure. Sounds great."

David stood from the table and began to walk out of the kitchen.

"You dropped something," Jim said.

His grandpa held a small black book. "It must have fallen from your pocket."

David froze.

He'd forgotten all about the notebook. He grabbed it, trying hard not to look conspicuous. It was a moment of truth. In his room, he opened the notebook to inspect the inside front cover. Written in penmanship that would make a grade school teacher blush was the name Christy Mathewson.

CHAPTER 8

WHEN JIM GOT THE JOB offer, he didn't have to think twice. It would be difficult leaving family and friends, but he and Catherine were newlyweds. At twenty years old, the excitement of moving to the west coast was palpable. A family friend had tipped him off to an opportunity in California to work for a large developer along the southern coastline. An untapped area basking in beauty and chance. With five hundred dollars in his pocket, and suitcases brimming with optimism, Jim and Catherine said goodbye to Chicago and headed west with nothing else. Catherine had relatives in Newport Beach who agreed to house the newlyweds until they got their feet planted.

They never had a honeymoon. On the way west, Jim promised his bride they'd spend a night in Las Vegas. For a couple of Midwestern kids, they couldn't believe the glitz of sin city. It only took Jim an hour at a Golden Nugget black jack table to burn through the five hundred dollar stash that would take them through to California. Catherine wasn't amused and Jim felt terrible.

Ducker's Pawnshop was located just off the strip. Tad Ducker provided a service for those who were down on their luck, and in this city finding people that fit that description was as easy as shooting fish in a barrel. Jim entered carrying a shoebox under his arm. He was stunned at the amount of jewelry scattered across the shop. There were guns, paintings, silver, fine china and statues. He even saw a set of dentures in a mason jar. He'd never seen anything like this, but desperate times called for desperate measures.

Tad Ducker was as dry as the desert sand. He was a lazy man with a wad of tobacco in his cheek the size of a plum. In the thirty years of having a pawnshop he'd seen just about everything come through his doors. He was not easily impressed. Jim approached Ducker and placed the shoebox in front of him. Ducker removed the lid with his thick freckled fingers to see what was inside. He picked up the baseball and looked at it like he'd never seen one before and asked what the relevance was.

Jim explained it was the one Babe Ruth hit out of Wrigley Field during the 1932 World Series; the ball from the famous called shot. It would have helped if Ducker had any semblance of baseball knowledge, but he didn't. After giving his best sales pitch, Ducker looked at Jim with a blank stare. He couldn't have cared less. "Son,

I was born in the day, just not yesterday. This means nothing to me. I suggest you pack up your little baseball and run along,"

"So there's nothing you can give me for this?" Jim pleaded. "It's gotta be worth something. I've got a job lined up in California. I'll be back in a couple of months to get it back. You've got my word that it's real."

"Boy, I don't even know you. What's your word mean to me? C'mon, this is just a scuffed up ol' ball and nothing more. I'm sorry."

Jim would never forget the humiliation he felt that day. Tad Ducker was just the first in a long line who'd scoff at the provenance of the ball's authenticity. Forty-four years later the doubt surrounding the baseball existed more than ever in Jim's mind.

He sat alone in the ice cream parlor reminiscing about his honeymoon, staring into the empty glass mug at the remnants of his root beer float – a tradition he shared with Catherine on every anniversary. It seemed like yesterday he and Catherine married. Memories from that trip to Vegas and Duckers pawnshop all seemed so vivid, like so many others he kept near his heart.

He checked his watch and remembered he told David they'd barbeque steaks. He placed a couple of bucks on the bar. He winked at the young girl with ice cream stains all over her apron and mouthed, *thank you*.

Across the lake, lights began to dance in the windows of homes like fire flies on humid Midwestern nights. Along the quiet walk home, Jim's mind drifted to more memories of Catherine and the life they shared. He missed her so much.

CHAPTER 9

THE NEW DECK WAS A ruse to circumvent his writer's block and he knew it. It sounded like a good idea at the time; sitting under the stars with nothing but beauty. The freedom of the outdoors, and breeze off the lake, would stoke his inner-most thoughts. Pages would flow like the wine from his bottle – at least that's what he thought. But outside of a few dinners with Stan and Martha, he hadn't stepped foot on it once for its intended purpose.

Adirondack chairs were poised at the edge of the deck where Jim and David enjoyed the unobstructed view of the moonlight across the top of the lake. They'd just enjoyed a delicious steak dinner. Piano music escaped through the screen door adding to the peaceful sound of night.

"She loved the piano so much," Jim remarked. "Today was our anniversary."

"How many years?" David asked.

"Would've been forty-four."

"What was she like?"

"You see how the moon lights up the entire lake? That's what she was like. There aren't enough adjectives to describe her. She was lovely, plain and simple. Everybody adored Catherine."

"Did she like baseball, too?"

"Not particularly. But she knew how much I did and never tried to get in the way of that. She loved the fact that your dad and I had a bond with the game. It made her happy."

Jim studied the last bit of wine in the bottom of his glass, swirling it before pouring it down the hatch. "What did you do today?"

"I spent the day reading."

"*Really*? Good for you. What did you read?"

"I went through a bunch of your books and ended up settling on one about Christy Mathewson."

"Wow. Now I'm really impressed! What was the inspiration behind that?"

David gazed into the openness. "I have to say, I took your lecture about the First Class to heart. Seeing the plaques and the history of it all up close has really got me interested."

"Well, good for you. You picked a good one to start with. He was a gentleman."

"The *Christian* Gentleman!" David added.

Jim smiled.

"Do you have a favorite from that class?" David asked.

"Oh, that's tough. I'd probably have to go with Ruth. He was in a league of his own. You see, David, this is the great thing about baseball. It's conversations like this that keep the game alive. No other sport has this kind of history – they just don't. Nobody sits around and compares stats from football or basketball players from a hundred years ago. But baseball is unique and I believe it always will be. But it also needs your generation to promote its incredible history going forward. And I worry that with everything else going on, and all the other distractions, kids your age are losing interest. Seems like you're developing quite a passion for it! Keep it up."

Banks walked over and put his head in Jim's lap. "I think somebody's telling me they want to go to bed."

David chuckled.

Jim stood and patted David on the shoulder. "I'm gonna hit the hay. I've got an appointment in Albany tomorrow. I'll be gone before you wake up." He walked across the deck and stopped halfway. "David, I know this whole thing is kind of awkward for you...for both of us. I want to do everything possible to make your stay comfortable. So if there's anything you'd like to do while you're here, just tell me."

"OK. Thanks."

"No, thank you. I needed this tonight," Jim said as he walked inside the house.

David remained in his chair captivated by the moon's superlative glow. He thought it was strange that his grandpa didn't invite him to come along with him on his errands in the morning, Christy Mathewson and his words hung in the air, "You never know what you're going to see or hear." He was right, the view was magnificent. He removed the notebook from his pocket and began to sketch the lake and the moon while the delicate piano notes, or maybe even whispers from a grandmother never known, filled his ears.

CHAPTER 10

THE OUTDATED *TIME* AND *NEWSWEEK* magazines scattered across the table in the waiting room were of no interest to Jim. His other option was to engage in a staring contest with the little girl in the floral summer dress. She sat next to her mother without a care in the world. Her mother, however, appeared anxious, a feeling Jim knew all too well every time he entered Dr. Tenney's office. He closed his eyes and waited for his name to be called. Within minutes he fought the urge to fall asleep as images from games he had attended clouded his thoughts; the different ball parks, the players, the shoe string catches and towering home runs. He began to relive personal anecdotes told to him by players he'd met over the years at the Hall. The thoughts kept coming and with clarity. He wished more than anything he could be at his computer, writing what he saw in his mind's eye instead of waiting to hear news he already knew. And then he remembered that night in the bar at Camilli's, when that faceless man said something so profound. *"Give him a piece of yourself, and in return maybe he'll give you what you need."*

That's it.

It took David's unexpected visit and the words of a complete stranger to give Jim the perspective he needed. In that moment, he realized he was writing the wrong book. He removed a receipt from his pocket and wrote down the perfect title. He couldn't wait to get started.

"C'mon in, Jim."

Jim looked up and saw Dr. Tenney's assistant, Anne, holding the door open with a clipboard in her hand.

"How are you today?" she asked.

Jim stood and smiled at the little girl in the floral dress. She stuck her tongue out at him. He stuck his out at her, and the girl's mother forced a smile. "All things considered, Anne, just fine," Jim replied. "I couldn't be better.

The garage was a dilapidated shack about fifty feet from the side of the house, surrounded by low hanging trees that kept it shady most of the day. The roof was in desperate need of new shingles, rotted by moss and years of harsh winters. David approached the side door. The rusted doorknob was jammed, frozen shut from lack of use. He pulled hard, and as it opened the smell of dust, and damp, stale air escaped at the first opportunity. He ran his hand over the wall trying to find a light switch, but couldn't. He took a couple of steps inside but froze when he felt something from above brush against his face. It was a thin pull chain dangling from the rafters. He pulled the chain, but nothing happened. The light bulb had been burned out for months, maybe more. His eyes began to adjust to the black surroundings enough to notice a large object in the center of the garage with a canvas cover. Whatever it was left a sliver of space to walk past. He unlatched the locks from inside the garage and pushed the large door up, allowing the outside light to creep in.

In the center of the garage was a boat. Just beneath the canvas cover, were the words *Master Craft* in a sparkling blue glitter stripe with white stars placed evenly about. He pulled the cover back exposing a clutter of camping gear: sleeping bags, tents, water-skis and other random outdoor accessories that filled the entire boat.

There was a built-in work bench along one of the side walls. Tools were scattered all over the work space. Boxes were stacked on top of the bench – sometimes three high – leaving no room to work. There was a pegboard wall above the bench with framed pictures hanging on it. David grabbed a flash light off the bench and shined the beam on the wall. His grandpa stood on the end in every one of these baseball team pictures. He looked much younger, more muscular and confident. There were six frames all together: Yankees, Cubs, Tigers, Angels, Dodgers and Yankees again. In all six photos father and son stood side by side bearing witness to the enduring bond they shared.

A wave of panic rushed over David when he heard his grandpa's automobile turn up the gravel driveway. Something about the garage seemed off-limits. He thought he'd try to close the large door and sneak out, but it was too late. Jim rolled up to the door and turned off the engine.

"I knew you'd find it sooner or later," Jim said.

"I didn't know you had a boat," he replied.

Jim let Banks out, who jumped down to greet David.

"It was your dad's."

"Really?"

"I've had it for all these years and only used it once or twice."

"How come?"

"I don't know," Jim said. He entered the garage and ran his hand over the smooth hull. "No one to go out with I suppose."

"You were a good dad," David said, pointing towards the Little League pictures.

"Coached every team he was on until high school," Jim replied.

"My dad was lucky."

"I have no doubt he would have done the same for you." David smiled.

"I meant to ask you something last night," said David.

"What's that?"

"When I walked into your office the other day with Martha you seemed upset. Something about a baseball?"

"It's a long story. How about I fill you in another time? I think we ought to go inside and see what our lunch options are. By the way, I need to go to my office tonight. You wanna tag along?"

David thought of the vault. "Yeah, sure."

Jim pulled on the large door and eased it to the ground. Banks was already half-way to the front door and the two followed. "Do you remember last night when you said if there was anything I wanted to do, just ask?"

"Yes," Jim replied.

"I want to take the boat out with you."

Jim laughed. "I knew that was coming. I'll tell you what, you clean out the inside and polish her off, and I'll take her in for a tune-up. Before you go back home we'll take her for a spin, deal?"

"Deal!"

CHAPTER 11

⁓

JIM WAS EXCITED TO GET started on his new book idea. He had some old notes and things he wanted to go through in his office, and told David to meet him by the entrance at ten o'clock sharp. This didn't give David much time to find out whether his meeting with Christy Mathewson was a dream, or a supernatural experience. He climbed the staircase to the second floor and hustled to the back of the exhibit where the elevator was behind the partition. He pushed the down button and waited. When the door opened, he stepped inside with a sense of purpose and pressed B for basement.

The elevator door opened and David darted straight for the vault. His heart thumped as he waved the access card over the black security pad. The lock clicked. He checked the long hallway to make sure nobody was there, then walked inside. The room seemed more disorganized. There were boxes and other collectibles out of place, left on rolling carts. It seemed unusual, and, left him edgy.

Maybe somebody was on their way back, or perhaps even still inside.

He cleared his throat intentionally loud.

"Hello."

No answer.

He searched the wall full of boxes until he found the one he was looking for. It was up high and out of reach, towards the far end. It had COBB written on the lower right corner. There was a step-ladder leaning against the shelves that he used to bring down the box. He removed the lid and inside was a gray jersey with pointed collars. It had four buttons down the center. On the left chest was a navy blue Old English D that hadn't changed in a hundred years. He lifted it from the box and let gravity unfurl the long sleeves. Just as he was about to slip his arms inside he paused.

What if?

Until now, he hadn't given any thought to the notion of it not working. He assumed that if it happened once, it would happen again. But if it was real, and he actually *did* travel back in time, it created a whole new set of circumstances. How long did it take to travel back and return to the present? He didn't pay attention to that the first time. Was it one minute or one hour in real time? He glanced at the clock on the wall. It was 9:48. He had twelve minutes to find out.

He put the jersey on and waited.

The room went black.

THE GEORGIA PEACH

A dim yellow light hung from the ceiling on the opposite side of the room. Standing beneath it was an older man with his back to David. He was folding gray flannel uniforms and loading them into an oversized trunk. The words DETROIT TIGERS were stenciled across the side in faded white paint. The man wore a worn out white tank-top tucked into khaki trousers. The room was hot and lacked circulation, leaving a rank smell of body odor mixed with moth balls and wintergreen rubbing liniment. The man didn't seem to notice David standing in the opposite corner of the room.

David wore a gray jersey that extended well beyond his elbows. The collar was stiff and irritated the back of his neck. It had an Old English D on the left chest that nearly took up the entire side of the shirt. His wool pants were too big, and his stirrups were heavy and dense.

How do guys play in these, he wondered.

He kept his eye on the man folding jerseys as he opened the door to an adjacent room. There were rows of lockers with short three-legged stools in front of each one. Suits and fedoras hung on rusted hooks. There was a large table in the center of the room with playing cards and Coca-Cola bottles scattered about. The sudden roar of a large crowd stopped David cold. It emanated throughout the clubhouse like a shockwave. A mixture of boos and insults were hurled at somebody with the intensity of a crowd gathered for a public execution.

Sunlight split the open doorway that led to a long runway outside the clubhouse. David walked towards the light as the intimidating taunts from above continued. He spotted a calendar on the wall next to the door.

MAY 1912

He hadn't noticed he wore spikes until he began to walk up the enclosed runway that stretched out before him. The crackling sounds of metal on concrete popped like embers in a blazing fire. Just then a man appeared at the top of the runway – a darkened silhouette from the radiant sunlight behind him. He walked towards David, his spikes making the same clattering sounds.

David stood still, nervous.

The hallway was cold and narrow. There was no way to avoid the larger than life figure walking towards him. Within seconds the wiry man stood only a few feet away. His steely eyes squinted at David like they were trying to penetrate steel. David couldn't talk even if he'd wanted to – his tongue was stuck to the roof of his parched mouth. Standing in front of him was Ty Cobb.

"What are you looking at? Cobb asked.

"Nothing," David whispered.

"Shouldn't you be up there helping the fellas out? They've been looking for you."

David hung his head. He couldn't bring himself to look at the intensity of Cobb. He focused on the thick clumps of brick dust caked on his pants, and the bat he held in his left hand. Cobb continued past and disappeared into the clubhouse. David paused and followed close behind.

Cobb was visibly angry, pacing back and forth in front of his locker when he noticed David in the doorway. "I've about had all I can take. From the moment I stepped foot into a big league clubhouse I've been ridiculed. Damn it, that loud mouth had it coming to him."

David looked behind him to see who Cobb was talking to. There was nobody there.

"What happened?" David asked.

"I just licked a fellow in the stands. I couldn't take it anymore. When he started in about my mother that was it! Not to mention I had Crawford and Delahanty giving me jazz, calling me a gutless no-good unless I did something about it. I don't even remember climbing into the stands. I realized after the fact that the SOB didn't have any hands. Probably wouldn't have stopped me anyway. Of all people, Crawford should know better than to call me gutless. I had enough of his act a few years ago when I finally challenged him in front of everybody. He wanted no part of me. Go on. You'd better get up there and do your job instead of sitting down here listening to me."

"But I want to be here," David replied. "I want to listen."

Cobb walked to his locker and removed a piece of wood that had a large bone mounted to it. He placed the bone on the table next to David.

"What is that for?" David asked.

Cobb removed a plug of chewing tobacco from his back pocket. He took a large bite out of it and threw the remnants on the floor. He held his bat out in front of him and inspected the grain like he was reading small print. He worked up a mouthful of spit and drenched the barrel with thick brown juice. He pushed the bat over the top of the hallowed bone with the precision of a surgeon. David watched like a boy watching his father handle a task fit for a man. "What are you doing?"

"It's called boning the bat. I'm smoothing out all the areas of the grain that have begun to split. It preserves the bat."

Cobb stared at the grain, inspecting every square inch of the barrel's surface. He applied another healthy dose of brown spit and began the process all over again.

"All I ever wanted was to impress my dad. I wasn't much older than you when I left home in search of my dream."

David was intrigued at the mention of Cobb's father.

"Was your dad supportive?"

"Daddy wanted me to be a scholar. I could have gone to any school I wanted. But I wanted to play ball. That's when I got an invite to join a spring practice for the Augusta ball club of the South Atlantic League. He tried to talk me out of it, but I wasn't gonna listen. He gave me six checks for fifteen dollars and told me to get it out of my system. I made the team, but after just two games I was released."

"Were you afraid to tell your dad?"

"Yes. But when I called him and told him of another opportunity with a semipro team in Alabama, much to my surprise he gave me his blessing. 'Just don't come home a failure' he said. After playing a few months and leading the league in hitting, the Augusta club wanted me back. I played for a great man in Augusta named George Leidy. There was one summer night when he came to my room and told me we were going for a ride. He lectured me in a fatherly way about taking the game serious. He told me that if I sell myself short, others will too. He wanted me to know that every boy in America would be idolizing me someday; that I would go down into the history books. But not unless I stopped fooling around! His words really got to me."

"So I guess he was right."

"Well, here I am six years later with four batting titles," Cobb said. "That's why it irks me when people talk about me in an unfavorable light. I fought my tail off to get here. And I'm telling you all of this for one reason."

"Why?"

"Because if you want something in life you're gonna have to go out and get it." Cobb stepped away from the bone and took a couple of swings that cut through the clubhouse air. "Nobody's gonna hand it to you."

He grabbed the bone from the table and returned it to his locker. He proceeded to take a few more cuts. David was amazed at how easy he handled the heavy bat.

"I bet he couldn't be more proud now," David said.

"Who?"

"Your dad."

"He died right before I was called up to the majors. He never saw me make it." Cobb leaned his bat against the back of his locker. In that moment, David felt sorry for the most coldhearted player in the game.

"Sometimes I feel like walking away from it all and telling all the doubters where they can stick it."

"But you can't," David said with a sense of certainty.

"Oh yeah? Why not?"

"Because, you're Ty Cobb," David replied. "And that would change everything."

Cobb was speechless, perplexed by such a profound statement from such a young man. His tight lips acquiesced, and a thin smile formed across his hardened face. David reached into his back pocket hoping to find his little black notebook. To his surprise, it was there. He removed it as Cobb headed towards the showers.

"Mr. Cobb."

"Call me Ty."

David extended his hand. "Will you sign this for me please?"

Cobb grabbed the notebook and a fountain pen from table. He opened the book and inspected the first page. "I see I'm in pretty good company?"

David smiled, "Only the best, Ty."

"Don't ever sell yourself short," Cobb instructed.

He signed the book and handed it back to David. On his way to the showers he removed his gray flannel jersey and dropped it on the ground. Just like that, Ty Cobb was gone leaving David alone at the table. He looked at the jersey in a heap on the clubhouse floor. It appeared to be the same one he removed from the box back in the vault. He reached to pick it up, but before he could it was plucked out from under him.

"It's time to go now, kid," a voice said from behind.

It was the man who'd been folding jerseys. David recognized him from some other place, which at the moment seemed so distant and unsettled.

Where, he wondered.

He could hear the water from the shower hitting the tile floor. And then he couldn't see or hear anything.

CHAPTER 12

~

JIM PACED BACK AND FORTH in the main lobby. It was five after ten; he was becoming more impatient by the minute.

Where is he?

David appeared running down the ramp, muddled and out of breath.

"Sorry I'm late," he said.

"What were you doing?"

"Taking a trip back in time."

"This place will do that to you."

If he only knew, thought David.

There was a door to the side of the main entrance. Jim stopped at an alarm pad positioned eye level on the wall. David stood behind him, but close enough to see the four digit code Jim punched in: 2130. He pushed the door open, and they stepped outside onto a small stoop. Jim checked to make sure the door locked behind, and they continued down a few steps onto Main Street. It had rained while they were inside. The air was heavy; streets were moist. They walked towards Jim's car parked a couple of blocks away. The store fronts were dark, cluttered with baseball knick-knacks and other antiques waiting for another day of fans looking to spend handsome sums of money. Up ahead a street light flickered before burning out. And the tiny town was still.

"Are you always the last one to leave?" David asked.

"Yeah, pretty much! They got so tired of waiting around for me that they finally gave me the code to set the alarm."

"They must trust you a lot."

"They know how much I respect the game."

"When you're in there all alone do you ever handle any of the memorabilia?"

"What do you mean *handle*?"

"I mean you've got all that amazing stuff around you, do you ever pick up a bat or glove and wonder what it must have been like to use it?"

"No, I never do."

"Do you ever try on old jerseys?"

"God no," Jim said flabbergasted. "Some of those things are over a hundred years old. I'd be too afraid of one of them falling apart."

David became more enamored with it all; the town and all of its lore, the time spent with his grandpa and the idea of possessing an unexplainable gift. Now that he'd memorized the code to the Hall's alarm system, it would make things easier to continue his expeditions alone and under the dark of night when the ghosts from eras past seemed to wake up.

~

The Grandfather clock rang twice causing Banks' ears to perk up. Jim lowered his hand and scratched the top of his soft head; within seconds his loyal friend was back to sleep at his feet. The house was dark and the absence of the moon made the large study windows look like sheets of black granite. David was asleep upstairs, giving Jim the peace and quiet he needed to work on his new idea. He was wired from drinking two pots of coffee; stopping now to brew another would only slow him down. The words poured onto the pages with such a profound purpose; never before had it been so easy. Time had slipped away from him. His rhythm was interrupted by the sound of the big clock once again.

Ding. Ding. Ding.

Jim looked up.

Three o'clock.

He knew he was onto something special. But the coffee had worn off and his eyelids felt like they were being pressed together by a carpenter's vice. He went upstairs, stopping at the door to the room where David slept. He stared at him like he used to stare at Bill and then pulled the door shut and walked to his room. For the first time in years he felt fulfilled.

My uncle had a cattle farm just outside of Milwaukee. It was about a two hour drive that never seemed to agree with my mother's stomach. We would always drive with the windows down and the hot summer air blew steadily on my face in the backseat. At around the halfway point of the drive, we'd pull off and my dad would treat me to a chocolate milkshake. To this day they were the best shakes I've ever had.

I slept easy on those drives.

Some of my earliest childhood memories were at my uncle's farm. We had big family get-togethers where the women would gossip and cook while the men drank and played various games with gloves, balls and a bat. I was too young to know what they were doing. But I can vividly remember my father playing catch with some of the other men. He would throw the ball with remarkable ease and I always admired how good he looked doing it. I sat close enough to hear the ball literally hiss through the air.

My cousins and other kids from the area would be off playing childish games, but not me. I sat next to the men all by myself, studying them. And that is where I fell in love with the sound a ball makes when it lands in the pocket of a leather glove.

I remember one day after the men were done playing (I must have been five or six) my dad called me over. He thanked me for being a "good boy" and asked if I wanted to play catch with him.

I thought he'd never ask!

From Jim's manuscript

CHAPTER 13

A PAIR OF SQUIRRELS JOCKEYED for position on a low hanging branch in the maple tree. The lake was calm; the humidity wrapped David like a wet blanket. He thought about his mother and how much he missed her. It had been over a week since they last spoke; the longest period of time they'd ever gone without talking. There was so much to tell her, and he knew that she would not only listen, but believe his extraordinary stories. Somehow she'd be able to talk him through his confused state of mind and help him accept the unknown, even if it made no sense at all. But the thought of explaining it to his grandpa kept him up at night. It was hard enough trying to build a relationship from scratch with him, let alone try to convince him that he'd met Christy Mathewson and Ty Cobb. Even though he had their signatures to prove it.

He laughed at how simple the lives of two squirrels were. He stared at the lake, and soon it became a blur washed out by visions of blue skies over his neighborhood back home. As he closed his eyes in an attempt to doze, the silence was broken.

"Is that seat taken?" Jim asked.

David turned, startled. "No. Have a seat."

"You like it out here, huh?"

"I love it!"

"I knew you would. A part of me was thrilled when your mom called and asked to have you stay with me. I was excited that you'd get to experience this."

"A *part* of you?"

Jim winced. It didn't come out the way he meant it.

"I was scared, David. I didn't know how you'd respond being stuck with your grandpa who hadn't cared enough to pick up the phone and call all these years. I was scared to have somebody around me who'd remind me so damn much of your dad – I didn't know if I'd be able to take that. I've never been able to cope with his death. It's why I ran away. When I lost Catherine it was hard, really hard. But I had your dad and we helped each other through it the best we could. Let me tell you…it was hell! And just when things started to get normal, if there is such a thing, he was gone. When he died my soul was punctured and my will to live escaped like air from a balloon. I didn't know who to turn to or what to do. I was scared of what I might do. So I packed my car and started driving. I had no destination in mind. Cooperstown wasn't even a thought. In fact, I thought about Florida. We had a timeshare in Boca

Raton where we vacationed over the years – Catherine loved it there. And then one day I found myself in Iowa in a small town called Red Oak. I was filling-up at a service station when I noticed a dirty puppy stranded next to a trash can. He was looking for food, couldn't have been more than two months old. There was nobody else around except the attendant. When he told me the puppy wasn't his I picked him up and got him some food and water. Within five minutes I was calling him Banks, and for the first time in two weeks I smiled. For no apparent reason I changed course and began to head north. Your dad and I always wanted to visit the Hall of Fame. I can't help but think that it was him pulling me towards this place. All I know is that when I arrived into town and saw this beautiful lake, I knew this was where I was supposed to be. I checked into the Otesaga Hotel and spent the next several days looking for a house. I got lucky with the one I found. I moved in and became a recluse; leaving only to buy food and alcohol. That's also about the time I started to write, which is another story for another time."

Jim stood and walked to the lake's edge. With his back towards David he asked, "What are you doing tomorrow?"

"I haven't really thought about it," David replied.

"Do you want to take a day trip to Chicago?"

"Chicago?"

Jim nodded his head.

"*Why?*"

"I have something I need to tell you."

CHAPTER 14

THE CAB ROLLED TO A stop on North Clark Street in front of the famous red sign that read: *Wrigley Field Home of the Chicago Cubs*. Jim reached for his wallet and gave the cabbie a hundred dollar bill. "Stick around would ya? I want to take my Grandson around the ball park. I'll be about an hour or so."

"You got it mister," the cabbie said. He turned the taxi light off and grabbed his sack lunch from the passenger seat. Jim and David stepped out of the cab onto the brick sidewalk. It was just after one o'clock. With the exception of a few pedestrians, nobody was around. The Cubs were on the road leaving the area outside the stadium empty, which is exactly how Jim wanted it. "Just to give you reference point," Jim pointed up to the red sign. "That sign is directly behind home plate." He placed his hand on David's shoulder. "C'mon, let's go for a walk."

They headed down North Seminary Avenue, which splits from Clark Street and runs parallel to the third base foul-line. The day was perfect; much cooler than a typical June afternoon in Chicago. The towering sky was without clouds and possessed a blue so beaming, it seemed without end. They approached Waveland Avenue and stood underneath a sign that pointed to Gate K. "David, I probably spent more time on this street growing up than in my own living room."

Old tri-level homes lined the left side of the street. Across the narrow road jutting into the sky was the left-field foul pole; the arbiter of countless home runs and long strikes going back to the days of Hack Wilson and beyond. And then there was the old wooden scoreboard in dead center field; an enormous green centerpiece that never seemed to stand out as much as it did on this day.

"What are you thinking about?" David asked.

"The fun I used to have. Before home games I'd stand right there with my buddies," Jim pointed to a spot in the middle of the street. "We could tell when Ernie Banks was taking batting practice by the amount of balls that rained down over Waveland. I must have collected hundreds of 'em over the years."

"What'd you do with all of them?"

"Let's just say your dad grew up hitting big league balls for batting practice."

Jim and David walked freely down the middle of the street. They stopped half-way down and stepped back onto the sidewalk behind the left-center field wall. Like the sidewalk beneath, the walls surrounding the park were made out of red brick. David rubbed his hand on the wall.

"There's so much history here, huh?" he remarked.

"You have no idea. That's Sheffield Avenue up ahead. C'mon, I wanna show you something."

"What is it?"

"It's why I brought you here."

Waveland intersected with Sheffield, which ran behind the right field wall. They stood on the corner directly below the old *Chicago Cubs* sign. "It's amazing how small everything is," David remarked. "There's not even a parking lot."

"You gotta remember, this park is a hundred years old. There weren't a whole lot of cars back when these old stadiums were built. They were usually built on city blocks surrounded by homes. The ball parks were a lot more intimate than they are today."

They walked about thirty yards down Sheffield Avenue when Jim stopped. "This is why we're here, David."

"What do you mean?"

"That spot, right there, has been the center of so many questions and doubts for me over the years," Jim said, pointing to the middle of the street. Jim looked back to the intersection of Waveland and Sheffield and up at the rooftops as a flock of gray pigeons took off in formation over center field. He stood in the middle of the street like a crime scene investigator trying to piece together an unsolved mystery.

"Have you ever heard of the called shot?" Jim asked.

David shook his head, no.

"It's one of, if not the most, debatable moments in baseball history. It happened in game three of the 1932 World Series. The Yankees had taken the first two games in New York and the Cubs had their backs against the wall. There was a stiff breeze blowing out to right field on that day. Perfect conditions for Ruth and Gehrig! In the first inning Ruth belted a three run homer off Charlie Root. Gehrig followed with one of his own. There'd been a lot of jockeying between Ruth and the Cubs players. When the fifth inning came around the score was tied at four. Root had settled in, and when Ruth came to the plate he threw a first pitch strike to him. Cubs players all started yelling at him giving him the business. Root threw two balls and then one more strike. The players were all over him. Ruth loved it. He held up two fingers as if to say, 'that's just two strikes.' What happened next is where it gets dicey."

"What happened?"

"Some say, including Ruth, that he pointed towards center field, predicting to hit the next pitch for a home run. There is sixteen millimeter film that possibly tells another story. It suggests Ruth pointed to the Cubs bench rather than center field. Gehrig, who was in the on-deck circle, claimed Ruth shouted at Root, 'I'm going to knock the next one down your throat.'"

"So basically nobody really knows?"

"That's right...though I tend to believe Ruth!"

A city bus drove down Sheffield interrupting the flow of the story. It was followed by two teenage girls on bicycles with red, white and blue streamers coming off the handle bars. They smiled at David. He blushed and smiled back.

"I don't get it. We came all the way to Chicago so you could tell me a story about *Babe Ruth?*"

"No," Jim said. "The story's just beginning."

Jim sat on the low curb across the street from the right field wall. "I was in the back of the house. It seemed like our whole neighborhood was gathered in our living room. All the men were telling stories about my dad while they drank booze from his liquor cabinet. The ladies were talking about how sweet and helpful he was. My dad was everybody's friend. I hadn't eaten in three days and wanted to run as far away as possible. My mom walked into my room and asked me to come out and thank everyone for attending. I wanted no part of that. I'd just lost my father. She sat me down on the edge of my bed and for the first time since he died I began to cry. And then my mom handed me something wrapped in tissue paper. She said my dad had wanted to give it to me for some time."

Jim paused, fighting back his emotions.

"What was it?" David asked.

"A baseball."

"The one on your desk?"

"Yes"

"I don't get it."

A deafening silence ensued. "It's the ball Babe Ruth hit out of the park that day."

"The called shot ball?'

Jim didn't answer. He just stared straight ahead.

"You're kidding me, right?"

"I grew up just a few short blocks from here in the same house my dad grew up in. Like me, he would hang out around the ball park. In those days, kids would get to know the ballplayers; a lot different than today. When Ruth hit that ball out of the park apparently my dad happened to be the one to pick it up. Of course at the time, being on the outside of the stadium, he wasn't aware of the ball's significance. I suppose to him it was just another home run that landed on Sheffield Avenue. It wasn't until later that the home run became controversial and by that time nobody believed him that the ball was authentic. My mom told me that whenever he'd bring it up to friends or people in the neighborhood they'd all just roll their eyes. It got to the point where he never wanted to talk about it anymore, which is why he never even told me about it. And now nobody believes *me*."

"Why does it matter so much to you? *You know* it's authentic and that's all that should matter," David said.

"That's just it. I *don't* know if it is."

"What do you mean?"

"I've had so many *'know it all's'* over the years laugh at me when I tell them about the ball. It bothers me that my dad never told me about it. Why did my mom hand it to me when he was gone and act like he wanted to give it to me all along? I want to believe it. Oh you have no idea how badly I want to believe it. Some days I do, and others...."

"Others what?"

"Others I wonder if my mom lied to me to get my mind off of losing my dad. I can't tell you how many times I've had to defend that damn baseball and try to convince people it's the real thing."

"I say stop trying."

"That's easier said than done."

"Grandpa, did your mom know a lot about baseball?"

"Mom? No, not a thing! She was always busy playing bridge with her friends or volunteering at the church."

"Then why would she pick the called shot as a means to get your mind off of your father? How would she even know about that unless your dad told her?"

Jim put his hand on David's head, rubbing it back and forth messing up his hair. "Why'd you have to put it like that?" he said with a smile. "You're pretty intuitive. I guess I'll just never know one way or the other."

David wanted to confide in his grandpa about his experiences in the vault. He'd been putting it off for the right time. If there was a 'time and place', perhaps under the skies of Wrigley Field was it. Especially after what Jim had just told him.

David cleared his throat. "Grandpa, I've been wanting to...."

Jim looked at this watch and jumped to his feet. "Oh geez, we've gotta get going. I told that cabbie we'd be back in an hour." They stood and walked to the corner of Sheffield and Addison. "Do you want to grab a late lunch before we head back to the airport?"

"Sure, that sounds great."

"I'm sorry, you were going to say something before I interrupted you."

"Oh, it's nothing. No big deal."

～

In the summers our street was packed with kids. The girls would be playing hop-scotch or jumping rope. The guys would be playing marbles, trading baseball cards or engaged in ultra-competitive stick ball games. The moms in the neighborhood didn't like it too much when our pink Spalding balls smashed up against their windows, but we didn't care. We didn't have a care in the world back then.

I remember one particular summer we were experiencing a terrible heat wave. Captain Anderson from the local firehouse was kind enough to open the valves on fire hydrants on those extra hot days shower-ing us with cold water for a minute or two.

If you've never experienced that you're missing out!

On one afternoon the street was soaking wet thanks to Captain Anderson. I can still hear the sound of the cabs tires squishing as it rolled to a stop on the wet black top. We were in the middle of a stick ball game and it was my turn to hit. The cab stopped right next to our faded chalk home plate forcing us to wait. The doors opened and much to our surprise Billy Williams and Ron Santo emerged. They were larger than life. They'd just left the ball park and were dressed to the nines. Santo wanted to hit and asked for the stick. I handed it to him, no questions asked. None of us really had time to process what was going on. I think we were all in shock! I stood off to the side and watched. "Throw it in here, kid," said Santo.

Little Larry Lindell put some extra "stink" on the ball (it's what we called it) and it whizzed right past the Cubs third baseman, who swung and missed by two feet. Billy Williams broke out laughing. So did Santo. We didn't know whether to laugh or look the other way. But we could tell he was kind of embarrassed. "Here you go, kid, show me what you've got," he said and handed me the bat. "What's your name?"

"Jim Danly," I replied. "My dad says you're blue-collar just like him." I don't know why but it's the only thing that came to my mind at that moment. I had no idea what that even meant; I just felt like I needed to say it because I heard my dad say it so many times.

"Well your dad seems like my kind of guy. Hit one out of the park, Jim Danly."

In 1968 Denny McLain won 31 games for the Tigers. He later admitted to serving one up to his boyhood idol Mickey Mantle that same year which was Mantle's last. The Mick was at 534 home runs (tied with Jimmie Foxx) when McLean eased one over the plate. Mantle didn't miss and put one into the right field stands. The two winked at each other and never spoke about it until years later. He'd hit one more home run before calling it a career.

Well, on that summer day, Larry Lindell did the same for me. He gave me the best pitch I'd ever seen and I crushed the ball to next Thursday. Both Santo and Williams let out a roar, and for a brief moment I was the king of Chicago's North side.

They got back in the cab and it drove away down the wet street. We were so stunned by what had just happened that we abandoned our game (and the ball) and all ran to our houses to tell our moms and dads. I'd have to wait a while because my dad wasn't home yet. When he walked through the door later that night, I rushed him like a four man blitz. I told him what had happened and that I hit one out of sight – that Ron Santo and Billy Williams cheered for *me*. I don't think he believed a word of what I said. I wish he had come home early that day. He would have seen it with his own blue-collar eyes. He would have been proud!

From Jim's manuscript

The 1965 season was another laborious one for the Chicago Cubs. By July 25ᵗʰ they were 12 ½ games out of first place with no real shot of making a late season run for the pennant. It was a sunny and humid day. The Cubs had dropped the first game of a doubleheader to the Pirates, 3–2 in 13 innings. A lot of Wrigley's faithful departed between games making the prospects of finding a field level seat as easy as plucking low hanging fruit. My dad called in sick to work (something he never did) to spend the day with me at the ballpark. We chose a couple of seats behind first base that were drenched in sun. He wanted me to pay close attention to my idol, Ernie Banks, who'd been the Cubs first baseman since 1962.

In the top of the fourth inning, Bob Baily led off with a sharp single to left field. Manny Mota then laid down a sacrifice bunt and reached on an error by the pitcher, Bill Faul. With runners on first and second, the next batter up was Roberto Clemente. He hit a scorching line drive to Cubs second baseman, Glenn Beckert. The rangy Beckert snagged the ball and flipped to the shortstop Don Kissinger at second base to double off Baily. Kissinger then fired across to Banks who caught Mota off the bag in no man's land.

4-6-3...Triple Play!

The Cubs defeated the Pirates, 5-0 behind home runs from Ron Santo and Billy Williams. There were five, future Hall of Famers who played in that forgotten doubleheader on that bright afternoon. I waited outside the player's entrance after the game in hopes to get my favorite Cubs hat signed. I got more than I ever bargained for! When it was all said and done I managed to get everybody involved in the triple play to sign the underside of the bill: Bob Baily, Manny Mota, Roberto Clemente, Glenn Beckert, Don Kissinger and Ernie Banks.

Years later I gave the hat to my pride and joy, my son Bill. And like gum wrappers rolled into little balls or paper cups from an after game snack, the hat was left in a dugout after a midweek Little League practice never to be seen again—found presumably by some boy without the slightest clue of who the names were and why they were significant to the hat. And just like that—like all of the games ever recorded—it was gone; left for memory, perhaps the way the game and everything that accompanies it was meant to be.

From Jim's manuscript

~

CHAPTER 15

JIM LEFT A NOTE ON the table asking David to meet him at the research center at noon. He wanted to take him somewhere special for lunch. When David entered the research center, Jim was on the opposite side of the room talking with an elderly man. He didn't recognize the gentleman and thought maybe he should come back later. But Jim saw David by the door and motioned for him.

Bernard Kastner received the J. G. Taylor Spink award in 1983 putting him in an elite class of baseball writers. The retired scribe penned a bi-weekly column called *Bernie's Bits.* It was picked up by the AP and ran in papers across the country for over thirty years starting in the 1960's. Bernie had a way of getting players to say things that no one else could. His love for baseball began in 1939 when his father was the scoreboard operator at Tiger Stadium. The one and only time Bernie had the chance to watch Lou Gehrig play happened to be the day Babe Dahlgren played first base instead. He was heartbroken – but his dad assured him he was watching history in the making – and that made everything OK again.

The 85 year-old looked every day of it. Rain or shine Bernie wore pastel cardigans and chewed on cigars like a toddler gnawing on a teething cookie. He had a story for everything, and whenever he'd visit the Hall the staff would stop whatever they were doing.

"How do you do?" he said extending his chapped hand. "Bernie Kastner."

"Hi," David replied.

"Bernie's been covering this game since I was a kid," Jim remarked. "I used to sit on my front stoop and read his columns on humid summer nights with my dad."

"Oh yeah," David replied.

"His columns went beyond the games and into the players' lives. You felt like you knew the guys after reading a Kastner column. And not just the stars either. I really looked forward to those columns."

"Awe, you're a sweetheart, Jim," Bernie said.

"Do you have a favorite story?" David asked.

"A lot of people ask me that. Before I retired I'd tell them it's the one I haven't written yet. To tell you the truth, I've written so many of them, I couldn't even tell you."

David couldn't take his eyes off the mutilated cigar in Bernie's mouth. It was saturated from all the chewing. "How'd you get into writing?" David asked.

"Well, I couldn't hit, catch or throw," Bernie said laughing. "But I loved the game."

"And the baseball world is better for it," Jim remarked.

"What's the biggest secret to being a successful writer?"

"A Hall of Fame writer," Jim reminded him.

"I call it the three *gottas*. You gotta love what you're writing about. You gotta be a good listener. And most of all they've gotta trust you. Once you get their trust they'll tell you things you never imagined. Some of it not fit for print either."

David pulled his little black book out from his back pocket. He turned the first few pages over and wrote: Gotta - *Love Listen & Trust*.

"Looks like we have a reporter in the making," Bernie said with a smile.

"Who knew?" Jim replied.

David slid the black book back into his pocket and winked at the old Hall of Famer.

Yeah, who knew, David thought.

CHAPTER 16

~

THE LUNCH CROWD BEGAN TO form inside Camilli's steakhouse. When Jim and David entered they were greeted by the smell of fresh onion rings and clam chowder. Jim glanced into the bar and spotted Glenn rinsing glasses in the sink. He motioned David to follow. As they approached the bar Glenn, looked up.

"Hey there, Jim," he said. "This must be your grandson."

"Hi, Glenn. I'd like you to meet, David."

Glenn reached his hand across the bar. "How are you?"

"I'm good. Nice to meet you," David replied.

"What can I get you two?"

"Iced tea for me," Jim answered.

"I'll take a Coke please," David replied.

"Glenn's been tending bar here since he was about your age, David. I think he's poured a beer for every living Hall of Famer."

"And some dead ones, too!" Glenn said, laughing. "How do you like Cooperstown so far, David?"

"It's great. The Hall's incredible," David replied.

"You can get lost in there, huh?" Glenn put the drinks on top of the bar. "You guys staying for lunch?"

"Absolutely. That's why we're here," Jim said.

"Good. I'll get you a table by the window. And it'll be on me today."

"You don't need to do that, Glenn," Jim remarked.

"I know I don't need to. I want to." Glenn walked into the main restaurant and spoke to one of the servers. Within seconds Jim and David were being escorted to a small table near a window where they could see tips of white sails on Otsego. "This is perfect, Glenn. Thank you," Jim said.

"My pleasure. By the way, I've been meaning to ask you, how's that book of yours coming along?"

David looked at his grandpa.

"It's not really. I've shelved it."

"Don't give up on it, Jim. I think it could be good. Well, you guys enjoy lunch and I'll check back with you in a bit."

"You're writing a book?" David asked.

"I've been working on one for years but it was going nowhere. So I decided to scrap it."

"Was it about baseball?"

"It was about *the* baseball."

"The Ruth ball?"

"Yes, the ball and the 1932 Yankees. But no matter how hard I tried, the story just didn't come together. It never felt relevant."

"For you or the reader?"

"What do you mean?"

"Maybe you were writing the book to convince yourself that the ball was real, and that your mom told the truth all those years ago."

"You know something, you're very sagacious."

"Sagacious?"

"It means smart."

David removed his black notebook from his pocket and wrote down the new word.

"Well, you'll be happy to know that I'm working on something else instead. And don't ask me what it's about. You'll find out when it's done."

"Good, because with a word like sagacious you *must* be a writer."

They shared a laugh together and browsed the menus. "I have some place else I'd like to take you after lunch if that's OK?"

"Sure, that'd be great."

∼

There was a gate between two small box office windows under a large brick archway. The gate was open, and a narrow cement ramp inside the small concourse led up to the grandstands. The baseball field was empty and seemed so innocent under the afternoon sun. Doubleday Field was just off of Main and Chestnut Streets, enveloped by aged Victorian homes and a church with a steeple and trees that stood long before the field's namesake did. Jim and David walked up the wooden stands to the top row and took a seat in the shade directly behind home plate. It was a small ball park with favorable dimensions for a hitter with any semblance of power: 295-390-312. The view was magnificent.

"The Hall of Fame was dedicated in 1939. That same summer the Yankees played the Newark Bears out there in an exhibition game," Jim said, pointing towards the field. "The Bears were the Yankees Triple-A affiliate. That '39 Yankees team was arguably one of the greatest of all time. They had it all."

"They must have clobbered the Bears."

"Actually the Bears won, 5-4. That's one of the beauties of baseball."

"That was Lou Gehrig's last year."

"I'm impressed," Jim replied.

"Thanks. I saw Gehrig's locker in the museum."

"The following year in 1940, the Cubs played the Red Sox in what was the first Hall of Fame game. They were exhibition games held every summer up until 2008 between two major league clubs. This place would be packed. Over time they had to put in all the extra seats down the lines. The people of Cooperstown loved it."

"So why'd they stop?"

"They say the travel was becoming too much for the players," Jim said. "It's pretty sad if you ask me."

"This is really neat," David said. "Thanks for bringing me here."

"This has always been a special place for me. When I first moved here and didn't know anybody, I'd come out here and sit in this same spot. I'd spend hours staring into the distance thinking about life and death and the meaning of it all. That was a bad time. But this field, this *wonderful* field and the smell of the fresh cut grass, and the way the sprinklers would dance in the outfield at dusk brought me back. It was therapeutic, like going to church in a way, I suppose. Call me crazy, but over time I felt a strong presence out here and I knew everything was going to be alright."

Their conversation was interrupted by a father and his young son who walked onto the field. They each had a glove on their hand, and the boy was wearing a brand new Cardinals hat that was too big on him. The father instructed his son where to stand. They began to toss the ball back and forth in foul territory next to first base. He offered words of encouragement, and the boy's infectious laughter rang throughout the ballpark. It was a beautiful thing to watch.

David looked on with the slightest smile that masked an unspeakable jealousy.

"I've never done that," he said softly.
The message was loud and succinct.
"I know," Jim replied. "I know."

Our seats were right behind the visitors' dugout. I got them from a business associate who wasn't able to use them that night. And what a night it was – a beautiful Southern California sky with vibrant pinks and oranges that blended to perfection before falling to the color of night. For many it was just another game. The Angels were fifteen games out, the Brewers nine. The game was of no consequence. But for me, it was most memorable. It was the first game that I'd enjoy with my son, Bill. The tickets were offered to me earlier that day; I could pick them up at will call. I called Catherine and told her to have Bill ready, that I'd be home around four to pick him up.

I was thrilled and proud rolled into one.

We arrived at the stadium by four-thirty, gates opened at five. On the walk up to the stadium we could hear the organ playing from the inside. I miss the organ at ballparks today!

We handed our tickets to the elderly man at the gate. He wore coke-bottle glasses and had yellow teeth. He greeted us with a smile and said "Welcome to Anaheim Sta-

dium." I told Bill to keep that ticket forever. I kept mine; it was June 16, 1976.

When we got inside the concourse, just
before we made our way to the tunnel that
would open Bill's eyes to a whole new world,
I remember leaning down and saying, "Bill,
you are about to see the prettiest shade
of green you'll ever lay eyes on. You will
never forget it, either." That's something
my dad told me and he was right. To this day
I get excited going to a game and catching
the first glimpse of green from an escalator or tunnel as I make my way to my seat.

We took our seats and watched the Brewers take batting practice. Balls were flying out of the park with ease; the cracks
of the bat echoing like gunfire on a field
of battle.

I told him to pay close attention to
number forty-four.

"Why Daddy?"

"Because he's one of the greatest to
ever swing a bat."

By the seventh inning, Bill was fading fast. But I knew that we'd get one more
chance to see Hank Aaron hit. I also knew
that it would be the last time. And in the
top of the ninth, with one out and a runner

on first, Hammerin' Hank hit his 749th home run off of Paul Hartzell in front of only eight thousand people. As he rounded the bases my focus was on Bill. I'd seen Aaron hit many home runs. I wanted to make sure Bill was watching. Without the slightest concern for the fans behind me I lifted him up and put him on my shoulders.

"Remember this Billy..."

I don't know for sure, but I could swear that right before Aaron entered the dugout he noticed Bill on my shoulders and winked at him – at least I think he did.

Hank Aaron would only hit six more home runs before ending his illustrious career. But for the rest of time my son would always be able to say that he saw Hank Aaron hit a home run at his first major league baseball game. And that he was there with his dad.

From Jim's manuscript

Going into the 1985 season Pete Rose needed 95 hits to break Ty Cobb's all-time hits record. I checked the schedule during

spring training and noticed that the Reds
had a 3 game series in Wrigley starting
on September 6ᵗʰ. I watched closely as the
season progressed and felt pretty certain
that barring any injury, Rose would be
close to breaking the record during that
series in Chicago.

Boy was I right!

This was a once in a lifetime opportunity. I purchased two tickets for all three
games - paid good money too! Bill had just
started his sophomore year in high school.
I wrote a letter to his principal and explained my intentions for pulling him out
of class for a few days to travel to Chicago. His principal couldn't have cared less
about Pete Rose, or baseball for that matter. But he was nice about it.

Going into the series Rose needed 5
hits to break the record.

We sat in the second deck between home
plate and third base and watched every
pitch with a sense of purpose. The Reds
beat the Cubs in the first game, 7-5 and
Rose went 2-5 with a home run.

Cobb 4191, Rose 4189

The Cubs won the next day, 9-7, but
Rose went 0-4. We had an early dinner that

night at Gibson's and talked over thick steaks and shrimp cocktails the size of small bananas. I had rented a convertible and after dinner we drove along Lake Shore Drive. The wind blew through our hair and the dropping sun pulled vibrant blues from Lake Michigan. I showed Bill where I grew up. I also showed him where his grandfather was buried. It was a memorable night – I wish it lasted forever.

The switch hitting Rose primarily played against right handed pitchers and the aging Tony Perez would play first base on days lefties pitched. Our prospects of seeing Rose break the record looked bleak for that final game due to the fact that left hander, Steve Trout, was scheduled to pitch for the Cubs. But the baseball Gods must have been smiling down on us because Trout injured his arm the night before falling from a bicycle and was scratched for right hander, Reggie Patterson and Rose inserted himself into the line-up.

In the first inning Rose singled bringing him within one of Cobb. He singled again in the top of the fifth inning to tie the record. Bill and I were thrilled. We high fived each other at what we'd traveled so far in hopes to see. And there was still a lot of game left!

Rose grounded out to short in the seventh inning. In the top of the ninth the Reds were down by a run. They managed to get three straight hits off of closer, Lee Smith, to tie the game at 5. But Smith settled down and struck out the next three hitters he faced including Pete Rose. The Cubs failed to score in the bottom of the ninth and the game was called due to darkness and ruled a tie.

We were so close to witnessing history!

I ran into Rose several years ago during induction weekend. He was signing autographs on Main Street in Cooperstown much to the chagrin of Major League Baseball. I have to admit, part of me admired his pluck. I approached him and explained that my son and I traveled to Chicago all the way from California to watch him try to break the record. He got a kick out of that and signed a ball for me that said, "Missed it by one hit," Pete Rose.

From Jim's manuscript

CHAPTER 17

~

MARTHA WAS SITTING AT HER desk reading e-mails when Jim knocked on her door. She peered over the top of her glasses, closed the thick folder in front of her, and pushed it aside. "How was lunch?"

"It was great," Jim replied. "Hey do you gotta second?"

"Sure. What's on your mind?"

"I've got something I want to share with you."

"Is it the box of chocolates I saw on your desk earlier?" Jim smiled.

"What is it?" Martha asked.

Jim took a seat across from her desk and opened his leather briefcase. He pulled out a small stack of papers about an inch thick. They were paper clipped on the upper left hand corner. He went through them making sure they were in order.

"You, more than anybody, know how much I've been battling with my book," Jim said, thumbing through the pages.

"I think that's an understatement."

"I've been working on something new. Something different! It just hit me about a week ago when I was sitting in the waiting room for my Doctor's appointment."

"How are you doing, Jim?" Martha asked, concerned.

Jim ignored the question.

Martha stood and closed the door. She twirled the rod to the vertical blinds behind her desk, giving Jim a reprieve from the blinding light coming in.

"I'd like you to be the first one to read it. I want your opinion on whether you think I'm on the right track."

He stood and dropped the unfinished manuscript on her desk like a weight off his shoulders. "Feel free to take it home with you," Jim said. He began pacing, watching her read the title page, waiting for her reaction. She couldn't take her eyes off of the title typed across the center of the page.

"I haven't even read a page yet and I can tell you're on the right track."

"I think so, too."

"Well then, I think this is cause to celebrate. Have you taken David anywhere other than here?"

"Come to think of it, no."

"So what are you waiting for? I say we take him out and show him something other than baseball."

"What do you have in mind?"

"I've got passes to the Glimmerglass Festival. The *Music Man* starts at 7:30. I hear it's really good. Maybe we could take him to Fly Creek Cider Mill for some fresh cider beforehand. C'mon, Grandpa, there's more to life than baseball you know."

"There is?" Jim said with a smile.

"Yes, there is. Besides, it wouldn't hurt to expose him to a little culture."

"You're right. I really want to take him to the Farmers Museum, too. Think we can squeeze that in?"

"I say we cut out now. It'll be fun."

"Fantastic. I'll call him and make sure he's ready."

David stood in front of the house throwing an old tennis ball against the side of the garage. Banks was lying by the front door, tired from all the chasing he'd done. The Bronco pulled up the gravel driveway, and Jim waved for David.

"Are you ready to go?"

"Yeah, I'm ready."

David climbed in the back seat as Martha turned and smiled. "Now you get to see what Cooperstown really has to offer."

"You mean there's more to it than the Hall of Fame?" David replied.

"A lot more."

"Are we going to bring Banks?" David asked.

"We're going to be gone a while. I think we'll leave him here," Jim replied. He led Banks to the house and let him inside. He stood at the door with his back to the car for an unusual amount of time. On his way back to the car, he winced with considerable pain; catching the eyes of both Martha and David.

"Are you OK, Grandpa?"

"Yeah, why do you ask?"

"It looked like you were in pain."

"Nope, everything's good," Jim mumbled.

Martha seemed concerned and looked at Jim, but he ignored her gaze.

They drove on Route 80 with the windows down. Otsego Lake flashed in-between the trees and lush fairways on the Leatherstocking golf course, until Jim pulled into a small dirt parking lot outside the old cobble stone Farmers' Museum. Its doors first opened in 1944 and the museum housed thousands of artifacts from textiles and wallpapers to old farming tools. Behind it was a nineteenth century village complete with actual structures relocated from communities around New York State. There was an old blacksmith shop, general store, a tavern and doctor's office, as well as a schoolhouse and wooden church. David watched as a blacksmith pounded hot iron into the shape of a horseshoe. He learned how butter was made and even milked a cow. Before leaving, Jim insisted they ride on the Empire State Carousel; something he'd wanted to do since arriving in Cooperstown all those years ago – something only the company of a boy could inspire in him.

From there, they headed west on Glimmerglen Road towards the Fly Creek Cider Mill where they watched how cider was made. They indulged in fresh cups until their bellies were content. David bought his mother a glass apple Christmas ornament from the gift shop, and Martha purchased homemade caramels and fudge to take with them to the Glimmerglass Festival.

They set out once again under ominous clouds that arrived unannounced over the lake. Streaks of lightening split the dark sky in half, and raindrops the size of quarters splashed on the windshield.

"Wow, did you see that?" David asked.

"This is nothing," Jim remarked. "There are times when the entire sky will be lit up for hours, and you'd think the world was coming to an end by the sound of the thunder."

"You probably don't get thunder and lightning like this in California, do you?" Martha asked.

"No. I've never seen it like this."

"It won't last long," Martha opined. "By the time the musical is over it'll be gone."

Jim parked the car next to the opera house. It was a multi-leveled complex nestled off the shores of Otsego Lake. It was an ideal setting surrounded by trees and grass, with a small pond in front with geese that floated freely. They entered just before the rain came and took their seats in the orchestra section. David looked at his grandpa who patted him on his knee in acknowledgement. Martha wore a proud smile knowing she had assembled a perfect day. People filed in and the theatre was near capacity. David turned around to take it all in, but was startled when he noticed the old man who he'd met at the lake taking a seat in the upper balcony. They made eye contact as the theatre lights started to dim. He looked back once more to see him, but it was too dark. The show began with a musical number, but David's mind was preoccupied with the man in the balcony. It would be throughout the entire performance.

CHAPTER 18

JIM HAD THE DAY OFF, which provided the perfect opportunity for him and David to enjoy blueberry pancakes and fresh cider on the deck outside. They talked about baseball and how it had changed over the years. Jim was impressed with David's grasp on the game. "You're a quick study."

"It's hard not to be in this town," David replied. "Do you think the guys from the Hall's First Class would be great today?"

"Oh, absolutely."

"You do?"

"People often say that guys back then didn't throw as hard. That's bull! Tell that to Ty Cobb who once said Walter Johnson's fastball looked like a watermelon seed hissing as it passed by. He said Johnson had the most powerful arm ever turned loose in a ballpark. There's a wonderful poem by Ogden Nash titled *Line Up for Yesterday* – you should read it. In it he writes 'J is for Johnson…the Big Train in his prime…was so fast he could throw three strikes at a time.' Trust me, David, they threw every bit as hard. But pitchers are used different today. Back then a pitcher would go deep into the game, often completing it. Now you've got a fresh arm coming in every inning from the sixth inning on. So, in that regard, I think today's players have it tougher. But that's where it ends. I think players today are lacking in basic fundamentals."

"Like what?" David asked.

"I've seen more missed cut-offs and errant throws from outfielders to home plate than I've ever seen before. Hell, most guys can't even lay a bunt down. To all those who say the older players weren't as good, I say nonsense! I'd like to see today's player wear flannel uniforms and play all their games during the day in the heat and humidity. Have them use old gloves and heavier bats and play with balls that aren't wound as tight. Have them go without batting gloves, sweat bands, body armor, and helmets when they're hitting. Have them wear shoes with no arch support; unlike the form fitting cushioned spikes today where players have a new pair virtually every day. Have them play nine innings or more on an infield only drug *before* the game, not two or three times *during* it. Have them travel and sleep on trains instead of flying on charted airplanes. I can go on."

"I've never thought of it like that."

"Not many people do."

"Three strikes at a time! I love that," David said. He removed his little black book from his pocket and wrote Ogden Nash inside. He set the book on the table.

"From the little that I've read since being here, it seems writers were much more colorful with their descriptions back then."

"They had to be. There was no television. They had to paint the picture for the fans. By the way, where'd you get that little book?"

David ignored the question and asked one of his own. "Who was better, Mathewson or Johnson?"

"That's a hard one. But, if I had to win just one game, I'd go with Walter Johnson, hands down. His numbers are unbelievable. The argument can be made he was the greatest pitcher ever. And yet he was so unassuming. If you were born after 1950 you've probably never heard of him."

Jim walked to the edge of the deck. He leaned on the wood railing and took it all in.

"I never get tired of the view from up here. That lake is so beautiful."

"I really want to take the boat out there. Maybe I can clean it out today. Do you think you can pull it out of the garage for me?"

"I'd be happy to," Jim said. "I'll be going to my office tonight if you want to come."

"I'd be happy to."

CHAPTER 19

~~~⌒~~~

IT WAS BY FAR THE hottest day since David arrived. He'd never experienced humidity quite like it. He'd worked up a sweat waxing the last side of the boat. Jim sat in a fold-up chair under a tree with a dirty tennis ball in one hand, and a cold bottle of Budweiser in the other. Banks was spent from countless throws he'd retrieved and now rested, panting by Jim's side, occasionally drinking water from a scuffed blue bowl.

The inside of the boat was completely cleaned out; camping gear stowed in the garage. Once David put the finishing touches on the outside of the boat, she'd be ready to take for a ride. He worked his rag in a circular motion under Jim's watchful eye.

"That's it. I'd say you're almost done."

David stepped back and admired his hard work.

"I still have a little bit left to go."

Jim took a sip of his beer. David paused to finish the cold Coke he'd been drinking.

"Was my dad any good at baseball?"

Jim looked at the sky.

"He was better than good. Your dad could throw a ball through a battleship. He got a full ride to play at USC, and after two years he had the attention of every big league scout in California. Hell, they were coming to our house for dinner. He went away to Alaska to play in a summer league before his junior year. I got a call one night and I could tell something was wrong. He told me he really hurt his arm. The MRI showed a torn ligament in his pitching elbow, the surgery sidelined him for a full year. When he did finally pitch again he was in the fifth inning of a game against Bakersfield with nine strikeouts. He heard it snap again. In the blink of an eye his career was over."

David took a seat on the ground next to Banks underneath the tree. "What did he do then?"

"He went through a period of depression. He pushed everybody away, even your mom who he'd just started dating. But she didn't give up on him. She'd stop by the house to check on him, and was always there to pick him up. She encouraged him to keep going. Your dad was a smart guy, really smart. School always came easy for him. He had a gift with people, too. Everybody liked him. But he was also tough as nails. Nobody was going to push him around. Those two traits helped him going forward. He made a few contacts from his college days, and after school he took a job selling pharmaceutical equipment. Within two years he was the top salesman in the company. Before long he was promoted to national sales manager. He married your mom soon after and bought the nice house in Irvine...bought this boat too."

"I didn't know any of this. Mom doesn't talk about my dad much. I had no idea baseball was such a big part of our family."

"Yep, I'm afraid it's in your blood," Jim said.

"Would you mind if I took one of those Little League photos in the garage home with me? I'd really like to have one."

"Please do. Take them all."

Jim stood and smoothed dirt with his foot when suddenly he let out a weak groan, bending ever so slightly at the waist.

"Are you OK?"

"Yeah, just a little cramp, that's all. Must be the heat," Jim said. He walked towards the house. "Keep going on the boat. You're almost finished. I'm going inside to cool off before heading to my office." Jim flipped David the tennis ball.

David held the ball in his hand and thought about his father, *the pitcher*. Doing his best impression of an ace he wound up and fired the tennis ball against the side of the garage. Jim watched from inside, behind the screen door, and thought about all the lost opportunities. David picked up the rag and continued cleaning his father's boat.

CHAPTER 20

~~

CONCEDED TO BE THE FASTEST *ball pitcher in the history of the game!* That was the first line on Walter Perry Johnson's plaque at the Hall of Fame gallery. David stood next to the wall dedicated to the First Class. He studied the bronzed faces that stared back at him and the millions who've passed by since the doors first opened. The more time he spent in Cooperstown, the more he realized how right his Grandpa was. *They* were the men who plowed the fields to grow the game into what it had become.

It was after ten o'clock. Jim was alone in his office, writing. His fingers raced across the keyboard against a mortal deadline. David had become used to walking the halls late at night. In an odd way, the exhibits kept him company and gave him solace like a child's imaginary friend. He stepped on the elevator and leaned against the back wall. The elevator descended. He thought about it all and what it must mean. There had to be a reason why he was chosen to go

123

back in time. He approached the vault door and waved the access card across the black pad. And like the previous two times it opened on demand, and a rush of cool air washed over him. He checked the clock. He had a half an hour. Plenty of time!

There was something bizarre about having incredible pieces of history laid to rest in gray boxes. He scanned them, noting several he'd like to open, but they'd have to wait; maybe another night. He spotted the one he was looking for and brought it down from the shelf. This jersey was unlike the others. It was all white with longs sleeves, and the front was void of any city or team name. On each arm below the shoulders was a navy blue W. Inside the collar in chain-stich was Johnson '24. He lifted the jersey out of the box and slipped his arms inside.

He took a seat on a stool and waited. Soon the blurred vision began and feelings of losing consciousness set in. He closed his eyes, inhaling deeply. There was a voice, almost a whisper, drowned out by a strong wind. He reached for it in his mind wanting it to be louder. The voice and its inflection seemed more than familiar. He had heard it before, but when and where he couldn't recall.

The voice called out for him.

And then again.

And everything went black.

THE BIG TRAIN

A group of reporters huddled together like a pack of dogs outside the clubhouse door. In between smoking cigarettes and scribbling notes, they spoke in muted tones about how nervous he was. David inched closer to glean to whom they referred when a voice from the top of the runway echoed off the cinderblock walls. "Somebody find Walter. We need him up here in five minutes." The reporters scurried up the runway for the field, leaving David alone.

The uniform hung under David's skinny arms like a sagging porch hammock. His baggy flannel pants were two sizes too big. He pushed the clubhouse door open and walked inside. It was a modest room that smelled like a mixture of body odor, burnt coffee, and cigarette smoke. Narrow lockers covered the walls. Two rickety ceiling fans cut through the stillness. Across the room was an open door leading to a smaller room. The smaller room had a large table in the center. There were ointments, gauze pads, and rolls of tape stacked on a silver tray at the base of the table. Standing next to it was a large man buttoning his white flannel jersey that hung well below his waistline. His expressionless gaze stared back at him from the full length mirror in front of him. He was tall and solid like an aged redwood. He had the most trustworthy face David had ever seen. He turned and noticed David across the room. "What do you need, son?"

David froze.

"Umm, Mr. Johnson, I just wanted to let you know that they need you out there in five minutes."

"Very well. I'll be there."

Johnson tucked his shirt into his pants and approached David with his cap in his hand. His bluish gray eyes were penetrating.

"Hold this for me, would ya?" David reached for the cap. The sweat stains under the bill were hard not to notice. The big man paced the clubhouse taking deep breaths and exhaling loudly. He was in no hurry.

"Is there anything I can get you?" David asked.

Johnson didn't answer. He walked to his locker and removed a small snapshot of his family from the top shelf and dusted it off. The clubhouse door opened and a middle-aged stadium usher popped his head inside.

"C'mon big man, they need you out there."

"I'll be right there," Johnson replied.

The room was silent but for the wobbling ceiling fans.

"Can I ask you something?"

"Go ahead." Johnson replied.

"You're nervous aren't you?"

"I've been pitching too long to be nervous," Johnson replied. He continued pacing in the clubhouse. "Well OK, maybe I'm a bit anxious, but don't you go telling anybody that."

"I would never."

"I may never experience another World Series again. I've worked my whole life for this. I owe it to the fans, and my teammates, to bring a championship home to Washington."

"What about yourself?"

"Myself?"

"Yeah, don't you owe it to yourself?"

He didn't answer.

"Aren't you going to get out there? They're waiting for you.

"I hear they've got something for me out there. Don't know what it is. I'm just not comfortable with all the attention, that's all. Why do you think I'm stalling?"

Johnson was in the last chapter of an incredible baseball story. At thirty-six, he'd been pitching in the big leagues almost half his life. Twenty-win seasons were as common as summertime; he had eleven of them up to this point. He'd gained the respect of greats like Ty Cobb, Eddie Collins, Shoeless Joe and Babe Ruth. But he'd never played in a World Series.

Father time was calling and he knew this might be his only shot.

"I can't explain it…but I've got doubt creeping in."

"Why now? You've pitched in so many games."

"Yes, but none bigger than this."

"Well, my grandpa told me if he had to win one game, he'd go with you over anybody else."

"Your grandpa sounds like a good man," Johnson said with a smile.

"He is," David confirmed.

Johnson put the photo back in his locker and ran a comb through his hair. He sat on his stool and laced up his spikes. David watched. He was amazed Johnson would even bother combing his hair at that moment. But that's what heroes do.

"They don't call you the Big Train for nothing," David said from across the room. "I say go out there and put your team on board. Take them to the promised land."

Johnson's lips tightened forming a subtle smile. "How is a kid like you so comfortable giving a guy like me advice?"

"I've been around great players. In their hearts they're simple men." David removed his black book from his back pocket. "Will you sign this for me?"

Walter grabbed the book. "You're a confident young fellow. Don't ever lose that, you understand? "

Confidence had never been one of David's strongest attributes. The absence of a father had left him unsure of himself at times. But perhaps being in the company of Hall of Famers had rubbed off on him. Maybe he was becoming more confident, because maybe, with a little help from his grandpa, Christy, Ty and now Walter, he was becoming a man. Walter opened the front page of the small book and saw the names Mathewson and Cobb. "Son, you *have* been around great players. Looks like I'm in pretty good company." He wrote his name beneath the other two in beautiful penmanship and handed the book back to David.

"Thank you," David said.

"No. Thank *you*," Johnson replied. "Where are you from anyway?"

David paused. "A place far away from here."

"Well then, I've got a game to pitch. Let's get out there."

There were men in three-piece suits, and heavy over-coats, standing around the Lincoln touring car. A large horseshoe wreath was placed over the hood with vibrant red roses. The car was a gift to Johnson from the fans in Washington. The mood was light. Packs of photographers swarmed around like bees to honey.

A U.S. Army band played behind home plate. A grounds-keeper tamped the batter's boxes with a heavy metal square, while another one watered the infield dirt by second base. Fans filed into Griffith Stadium to see their aging ace start his first World Series game. David watched autumn's shadow crawl across the outfield grass from the top step in the corner of the dugout.

The crowd began to roar with anticipation.

From the dugout he emerged, larger than life.

He was a living legend, when all he wanted to be was a pitcher.

Walter Johnson removed his hat and walked towards the Lincoln touring car. He gave a bashful wave to the thirty-five thousand in attendance, and the men in three-piece suits greeted him with firm handshakes and gregarious back slaps. Photographers knelt and began taking pictures. One after another flash bulbs popped. The always classy Johnson obliged by sitting on the shiny bumper of his new car, smiling ever so slightly until each one got what they wanted.

David watched from the top step of the dugout. He thought about his mother and the house he lived in, and how far away they both seemed from this moment. It was hard to fathom sharing time with the man everyone so widely applauded. He knew something about Walter Johnson nobody else in the ballpark did, and as a result he learned something about himself that would pave the way to his future. He began to clap for the hero when the two caught eyes for the last time. Johnson winked in acknowledgement, and like an old pro David just tipped his cap.

From off to the side a man with a long overcoat approached. He moved hastily, causing David to turn his way. He heard a loud pop followed by a bright flash. He put his hands up to rub his eyes; the light from the camera blinded him temporarily. The man holding the camera placed his hand on David's shoulder. "It's time to go now, kid."

Kid?

Time to go?

The bright light that had stained his eyes began to fade away but not before everything turned black.

CHAPTER 21

THE WATER LAPPED AGAINST THE side of the old row boat tethered to a rusted stake. The boat was made of wood painted maroon and white, and the word HEREAFTER was painted across the back. The inside was varnished teak and pristine. It was dark outside. The sleepy, dark, town was pardoned from the crowds of tourists who flooded the streets earlier that day – everyday. His footprints melted into the damp grass along the barren shore line. He checked over his shoulder to make sure no one watched.

His mission for this night was complete.

Arthur Page knelt and untied the rope from the stake and dropped the loose end into the water. He gave the boat a slight shove and stepped inside. He sat on the wooden bench as the boat began to drift from the shore into the calm Otsego water. He lit a cigarette and exhaled slowly into the night air, and then he began to sing an old favorite under the stars.

Where the blue of the night
Meets the gold of the day
Someone waits for me
And the gold of her hair
Crowns the blue of her eyes
Like a halo tenderly.

The lake was deserted but for the million reflections of moonlight. Arthur felt at ease on Otsego late at night when Cooperstown was asleep; when he didn't need to hide from who he was. He picked up the oars and pierced the surface of the water. He rowed himself towards forever as he continued to whistle his favorite song. Before long the whistling subsided. The peace and calm from the subtle splashes of the oars surrounded him until his boat disappeared into one of the moon's many reflections.

CHAPTER 22

JIM HADN'T BEEN ABLE TO sleep for hours. He couldn't stop tossing and turning. Sweat formed on his forehead, his stomach ached. He sat and took a big sip of water from the glass on his nightstand, not to quench his thirst, but to extinguish the fire in his abdomen. He'd been experiencing weird dreams of various colors and unrecognizable imagery. He didn't know how much longer he'd be able to hide this from David. He fretted having to tell him, but knew it was inevitable before David left for home. He walked to the bathroom and almost fell. The pain was extraordinary. A night light above the sink provided just enough of a glow to expose his vanquished face. He didn't recognize who he saw. He leaned over the toilet and began to vomit, pretending not to see the blood.

The only thing going to calm his stomach was a shot of whiskey chased by hot tea. The pain had grown worse over the past few months, inviting itself into his consciousness. He walked downstairs and stopped at the table where he kept his wedding ring next to a photo of

Catherine. He picked up the photo and stared into her eyes, and he remembered their last conversation as if it happened that night. She knew the end was near, but she didn't know it would be within an hour. She lay still in the bed Jim and Bill had placed in the living room. She was surrounded by candles and blankets knit by friends from all across the country; get well cards were lined in rows across the top of her piano. She'd never learned to play the piano, but always wanted to. She talked about second chances and what she'd give for one. Not in a self-pity wanting to travel the world kind of way. But rather, longing for more time to tell the ones she loved how much they meant to her. It was a simple wish. One she knew she'd never get the chance to see through.

She made Jim promise that he'd live out the rest of his days honoring her by opening up to those he loved; not just family, but friends. And then it hit him. He had betrayed her. Now that he was starting to build on something with David after all these years, he too was faced with the question of time. He turned the gas burner on under the kettle and reached for a bottle of his finest whiskey. He filled two shot glasses: one for him and one for Catherine. "To second chances, sweetheart," he whispered. He lifted both glasses into the air and closed his eyes. He put the empty glasses in the sink and poured himself a cup of tea before entering the study. It was almost 2 o'clock when the computer monitor illuminated. He began typing while thinking of his beloved wife and a particular friend he wished he would have talked to more.

I returned to Chicago in 1998 to meet up with my best friend from childhood, Anthony "Tony" Baroni. We had lost touch over the years. When I moved to California he moved to Myrtle Beach, South Carolina to open up a deep dish pizzeria. He called one day out of the blue. He had heard about Catherine and Bill and felt terrible that he didn't know sooner. It meant the world to me. He said we should meet up in the old neighborhood and go to a game. I hadn't been to one in the two years since they passed away.

We met behind the left field wall on Waveland. It's where we always met as kids. He was much heavier than the last time I saw him, a lot grayer too. It was early May and the day was overcast. There were about fifteen thousand people who made it a priority to watch the Cubbies take on the Astros. Tony picked up a couple of seats from an old contact he had. They weren't bad either. They were in the second deck between home plate and first base. Besides my dad, Tony was the biggest Cubs fan I knew. I love the Cubs, but Tony really loved them. Box scores every day, day ruined if they lost kind of love. And that meant a lot of ruined days!

I've been fortunate to attend a lot of games all across the country. But this is the only one where I can honestly say I had no care of what was going on out on the field. The players seemed like a blur to me. I was so engaged with my friend, laughing at old stories and crying about new ones, that I'd let the game get away from me. I knew there wasn't a whole lot of offense by either team — particularly the Astros. But I didn't put two and two together until the ninth inning as to why the fans were erupting with applause throughout the game.

"Jesus, Mary and Joseph (that was Tony's favorite saying) do you see what I see?" he shouted.

"No," I replied.

"Take a look at the K's out there in the bleachers," he said.

There were 19 K cards being held up by fans that were on the verge of going nuts. I had no idea. The most ever in a game was 20. Roger Clemens had done it twice. The National League record was 19. We were on the edge of history.

When Derek Bell walked up to the plate with two outs in the top of the ninth the place was buzzing. But for reasons I can't explain I couldn't hear it. It's like I lost my hearing momentarily. It was so loud it was quiet. The fans were waving their arms, clapping and pumping their fists but it was completely muted for me. When Bell swung through a slider on the outer half for strike three the place went crazy. Tony looked at me and shouted. I could read his lips. Can you believe that, Jimbo? No, I screamed back.

Cubs Win, 2-0. The players swarmed Wood out at the mound, congratulating him with hugs and high-fives. Before long the field was empty, erased like a grade school chalkboard.

Baseball is like art – it has 162 clean canvases everyday waiting to be painted with new memories and new records. It's what I love about the game. I never saw Tony again after that trip. He died from a massive heart attack on the first day of spring in 2003. I suppose if that didn't get him the Cubs collapse later that fall would have. I miss my friend Tony.

From Jim's manuscript

CHAPTER 23

DAVID NOTICED THE MIDDLE-AGED AFICIONADO sitting at the same spot at the long wooden table for the past few days. His face was long and narrow, masked by a dense salt and pepper beard. He wore horn-rimmed glasses that rested on the edge of his red bulbous nose. He was diligent, keeping copious notes in a wire-bound note pad. He never said much and would usually break for a couple of hours in the early afternoon, only to return until the center closed.

Stan had practically worn a path to the vault making countless trips back and forth at the request of the dedicated researcher; usually with a new cart full of photos and old articles of a certain player.

David sat at the end of the table with his black book in hand, and a copy of Ogden Nash's 'Line-Up for Yesterday.' After hearing the verse about Walter Johnson, he asked Stan to bring him a copy so he could read the entire poem. The simplicity of it was charming. It was written in 1948 and drew on each letter of the alphabet tying that letter to a major leaguer of the day and of the past. He wrote the following verses inside his black book in alphabetical order.

C is for Cobb
Who grew spikes not corn,
And made all the basemen
Wish they weren't born.
J is for Johnson
The Big Train in his prime
Was so fast he could throw
Three strikes at a time.
M is for Matty,
Who carried a charm
In the form of an extra
Brain in his arm.

It was half past four when the man packed his belongings into a leather satchel. He stood and dropped a pair of white cotton gloves into a basket in the middle of the table. "Thanks for all of your help, Stan," he said. "I think I've got all I need."

"My pleasure! I look forward to reading your book when it's done. It should be a good one!"

"I'll be sure to send you a copy for all you've done"

"Excuse me," David interrupted.

The man looked over his glasses.

"If you don't mind me asking what are you writing about?" David asked.

"It's a comprehensive book on all the great pre-war pitchers. I just finished compiling a lot of interesting tidbits about Walter Johnson!"

The mention of Johnson peeked David's interest. He zeroed in on the two folders on the table next to the man and wondered what was inside. He wanted to tell the man that he'd just spent time with Johnson, one-on-one, and that he had some interesting tidbits of his own. But he thought better of it.

"My grandpa says he's probably the best pitcher of all time."

"I can't argue with your grandpa," the man said.

"Let me know if you need anything else," Stan said.

"I appreciate that," the man replied. He stood and shook Stan's hand, and on his way out he turned and gave David a subtle wave.

Stan returned to his office and picked up his phone to make a call. David remained seated at the far end of the long table and looked over to check on his grandpa, but he had stepped out of his office unnoticed. David went over to where the man had worked and took a seat. There was a push cart next to the table with two large boxes on it labeled: Johnson. He put on a pair of white gloves and removed a folder from one of the boxes. Inside the folder were old black and white images. The first few were portraits of the big right hander, along with a terrific photo of Ty Cobb with his right hand on Johnson's shoulder, both with quiet expressions of admiration. There was even a family photo taken outside of Johnson's winter home in Daytona Beach, Florida where he posed with his wife and four children. David flipped to the next one in the stack and felt the hair on his head stand straight. As he studied the picture, his hands trembled and a burst of perspiration formed across his brow. There was Walter Johnson in his home uniform, men in three-piece suits, and a brand new car with a horseshoe wreath. And something otherworldly that nearly caused his heart to stop.

Oh my God!

Standing on the top step of the Senators' dugout wearing a baggy uniform was David.

"What do you got there?" Michael Witz said.

David stuffed the photo back into the folder as if he'd been caught doing something he shouldn't be doing. "Huh? Nothing!" he replied.

"Geez, you don't have to get all crazy on me. There's no harm in looking at photos. C'mon, let's see it."

David didn't like Michael from the moment he saw him argue with his grandpa over the baseball. Michael reached for the file. He pulled out the photo to see what he was trying to hide.

David held his breath. "Yeah, I know this shot. I love the expression on Mathewson's face," Michael said.

"Johnson."

"Huh?"

"That's Walter Johnson."

"Of course! I knew that. I meant Johnson. Trust me, rookie, you don't want to question my baseball knowledge."

"How many wins did Johnson have?"

Michael turned red. He couldn't believe the young kid was actually standing up to him.

"I know it was close to four hundred."

"Four hundred seventeen."

"All right you two," Stan said poking his head out from his office. "Michael, I've got a couple of carts in my office that need to go back to the vault." Michael glared at David and proceeded to walk into Stan's office. A few seconds later he exited with the carts through the back door.

David had to get rid of the photo. There was no way he could allow his grandpa and Stan, or anyone for that matter, to see it. In the middle of the table was a large coffee-table book on the World Series. He slid the photo inside the front cover and stood with the book under his arm. He poked his head into Stan's office.

"Can you tell my grandpa that I'm going back to his house? If it's OK with you I'd like to borrow this book. I'll bring it back tomorrow," David said.

"No problem, David. Hey, listen, don't let Michael bug you. He thinks he knows everything."

"I've noticed."

Stan winked and gave David a thumbs up.

He left the research center and didn't look over his shoulder until he reached the gravel driveway to his Grandpa's house. He opened the book and removed the photo hoping he'd be gone; like it was all some sort of mind game. But with one more glance it became all too real. He was as clear in the photo as Walter Johnson.

CHAPTER 24

⁓

THE CROWD ON THE STREET had all but dispersed as the sun fell behind the rooftops. David walked two blocks east on Main and headed up Chestnut to Doubleday Field. He needed some place to go and clear his mind after seeing the photo. The entrance was open, and he climbed the wooden steps to the top of the grandstands, taking a seat behind home plate. It was near dark, and he could smell the moisture from sprinklers that worked in unison to quench the outfield grass. He closed his eyes and let the repetitive sounds of spraying water drown out his nerves. *Chit…chit… chit…chit…chit…chit…chit-chit-chit-chit-chit-chit-chit-chit.*

Everything was different now. The photo with David and Walter Johnson posed a serious problem and hastened the need to tell Jim. There was no way around it, he had to come clean. Tonight would be the night he would tell him. He would go to the research center, walk right into his office, and blurt it out; whether or not he believed him was no longer his problem. It would be off his chest and he'd be able to enjoy his remaining days in town.

A man entered the ball park through an opening along the fence down the right field line. He knelt and began adjusting a sprinkler head in right field, near the warning track. He moved to the next one, and the next one after that. He was getting wet from all of the mist coming off each head, but it didn't seem to bother him. David watched from above – admiring the man's commitment to his job. There was something so peaceful about it; taking care of a baseball field at night with nobody around. Just before exiting he turned and looked to the top of the bleachers, like he knew somebody watched all along. By now it was dark and the man was all but a silhouette. He raised his voice above the sprinklers and said, "I'll be lockin' up soon, kid."

That voice…it's him.

The man from the point…the man in the balcony at the Glimmerglass festival…the voice that always sent him *back* from his trips to the past!

David shot up from his seat to get a better look. But it was too dark. He ran down the steps and out the main entrance. The parking lot was empty; not a car in sight. He ran to the right field foul pole where the opening in the fence was; his breathing more laborious with every stride.

He rounded the corner behind the right field fence expecting to see him. But all he saw were backyards with no fences, lush trees, big lawns, and a heavy lady sweeping her back steps beneath a dim porch light.

"Excuse me," David said, out of breath. "Did you see a man come back here?"

"I didn't see anybody. What'd he look like?"

"I'm not sure," David replied. He turned around and jogged back past the front gates and down the left field side of the ball park. What would he say if he found him? He didn't know. He waited close to thirty minutes next to a tree and an old tractor tire while the sprinklers continued to *chit-chit*. And the man never returned.

If was 9 o'clock on the button when David barged into the research center. He was short of breath and looked flustered. Jim was in his office with Stan, Martha and a man David had never seen before. He caught his grandpa's gaze and waved while mouthing the words *I'll be back*. Jim nodded and David left the room. He hurried for the elevator and took it down to the basement. He removed the access card from inside his notebook and swiped it over the pad on the wall. The door to the vault clicked open. There was an unintentional theme taking shape. First it was Mathewson, then Cobb and Johnson – all members of the First Class. He reached for the box that said Wagner in the bottom right hand corner and removed the lid.

David was past the point of being in awe when he opened a new box. He knew what to expect. It had become a mission of sorts, with the purpose still unknown. The jersey was the color of old white paint that had turned yellow with age. It had red piping down the front and said PIRATES in red block letters with a blue outline. Unlike the other jerseys this one had a zipper and inside the neckline it said Wagner '46. He removed it from the box and slipped his arms inside. He waited and nothing happened. He checked the clock on the wall. A minute had passed. He became nervous and wondered if he should put the jersey back. He started to unzip the old blouse when suddenly he lost his breath like the shock one gets from jumping into a cold pool. And everything went black.

THE FLYING DUTCHMAN

Snow fell with the intensity of a shaken snow globe. Piles of dirty ice were stacked in front of stores along South Bouquet Street. David had never been in the snow before. There was such a peaceful feeling. The only form of shelter was the green awning under which he found himself standing. Behind him were wooden doors with circular windows above long shiny brass fixtures. The red carpet he stood on was dirty, wet from the slush caked on by the patrons going in and out of *MacGillycuddy's*.

Why here?

The door opened and a voice behind him disrupted everything. "Let's go lad, get inside." David turned to see who talked to him. The heavy doors were held open by a short man wearing a thick sweater. He had a layer of gray hair on the back and sides of his head that made peach fuzz look long. He didn't appear to be young or old, but ageless and possessed a whimsical smile that left David uneasy.

"I've been watchin' you through the window for the past five minutes. You're gonna catch pneumonia standing out there like that. Why don't you come on in and warm up," the bald man said.

David looked once more out to the street, then back again at the man in the door.

"OK, thanks," he said.

The tips of his ears thawed the moment he stepped inside, and the man escorted him to a table with two chairs. "Can I get you some hot cocoa?"

"Sure. Thanks," David replied.

On the far side of the room was a roaring wood fire. Next to that was a long bar with men hunched over stiff drinks, not saying much. A bartender stood with his back to David, talking with a few hardened regulars. David surveyed the entire room. The walls were crowded with framed black and white photos of weathered men in factories and mines who all lacked smiles, but not desire. The parquet floor was long overdue for a shine, and three ceiling fans rotated slow, barely pushing away the stale cigar smoke that stuck to the air.

The bald man returned with a steaming mug of cocoa. "Here you are, lad," he said. "Take your time."

"Thank you," David replied.

Just then the wooden doors opened, letting in the white glow from outside. Standing in the doorway was a man who appeared to be in his early seventies. He was wearing a heavy overcoat and a black fedora he removed once he stepped inside. Though he was old he looked to be as strong as moonshine. He had a barrel chest and long thick arms with hands that could bend rebar. He hung his coat and hat on the rack next to the door and stood momentarily to take inventory of the room. The men at the bar all straightened up out of respect. David watched, curious by the man's disposition and the others' willingness to acknowledge it.

The man began to walk with a bowlegged limp towards David. His thin lips formed a smile, but were easily erased by an immeasurable nose that could cast a shadow on a sunny day.

"Mind if I sit down?" he asked.

"No, go ahead," David replied.

The old fellow sprawled back in his chair and let out a deep breath. His cropped hair was the color of vanilla ice cream, and his trousers rode up his outstretched legs exposing his swollen ankles.

"It's nasty out there isn't it?"

"Yeah," David replied.

"What's your name?"

"David."

"Where you from, David?"

"California."

"What are you doing in Pittsburgh? Are you a runaway?" the man asked followed by a chuckle.

"No."

The little bald man approached the table and placed a tall mug of ice cold beer in front of the old man. "It's on me, Hans. I brought you some warm nuts, too."

"Thank you, Liam."

"My pleasure," the bald man said as he walked away.

"He owns the joint," the old man said to David.

David sipped his cocoa, still observing the old man.

"So what brings you here?" asked the old man.

"You wouldn't understand."

"Oh, really? You think I collected all these white hairs by being an imbecile?"

"I guess not," David replied.

"Then what?"

"Don't laugh."

"Go on."

"I'm looking for the great Honus Wagner?"

"Here? At a bar in downtown Pittsburgh in the middle of a snow storm? Why are you looking for him?"

"It's just something I gotta do."

"And if you found him?"

"I'm not sure," David replied. "You see, it's kind of like a puzzle."

"A puzzle?"

"Yeah. I need to see him to complete the puzzle."

"I see," the man said.

"I've got this book," David removed the black book from his back pocket and slid it across the table. "It's signed by some pretty great players, and I really need to add Wagner to it."

"So let me get this straight. You came out in a near blizzard to try and have Honus Wagner sign your little black book? What made you think you'd find him here?"

"I'm not sure to tell you the truth. I just kind of ended up here."

The old man took a handful of nuts and shoveled them into his mouth.

"Do you ever feel like you're running out of time?" David asked.

"Look at me. I'm not getting any younger. But what's a young guy like you worried about time for?"

"I'm leaving to go home soon, and I've got to tell my grandpa something very important before I go. Having Wagner sign my book is really important to what I have to tell him."

"What's stopping you?"

"Stopping me?"

"From telling him whatever it is that's so important."

"I don't think he'll believe what I have to say."

"Have you ever given him a reason to doubt you before?"

"We've never had much of a relationship before. We're just getting to know each other now, and I don't want to risk the progress we've made by telling him something that might push him away. But I also want him to be happy and have peace of mind."

"What's preventing him from having it?"

"The answer to a question that's been troubling him for years."

"Is it one you can provide him?"

"I believe so. But having Honus Wagner add his name to my book would really help."

"Is there a wedge between the two of you?" the old man asked.

"A wedge? No, just a lot of distance! When my mom told me I had to visit my grandpa I was kind of upset. I wanted to stay home and hang out with my friends. My grandpa left us when my dad died."

"How long ago was that?"

"Almost sixteen years."

"You can't be much older than that."

"I never knew my dad. He died two months after I was born. I've really had nothing to do with my grandpa over the years and the thought of visiting was terrifying. But once I got to his house I began to see things in a different light. And it didn't take long for me to understand it all."

"You mean you forgave him?"

"Yes, I guess I have."

"Have you told him that?"

"No."

"Well, maybe you should."

The old man opened the book and inspected the names inside. "Do you follow baseball much?" David asked.

"As a matter of fact, I do. They don't come much better than these guys," the old man said referring to the names in the book. The old man took a pen from his shirt pocket and neatly wrote his name in the book beneath the other three names. "What are you doing?" David asked, shocked.

"Those fellas over there," the old man pointed towards the bar, "they all know me. Most of the time I'll put a fifty cent piece down on the bar and start telling stories. And before I know it, I'll have a crowd of people around me buying me drinks. And when I'm ready to go I just grab my fifty cent piece off the bar and head for home. It's great...saves me a lot of money."

"How come they want to buy you drinks?"

"I suppose it's what twenty-one years in the major leagues gets you."

"Honus," a voice called out from the bar. *"We're waiting for you. What are you drinkin' today?"*

"We've gotta spot for you, Honus," another voice shouted.

David looked back at the vociferous bunch and realized they were calling the old man across from him. "You mean *you're...."*

"Look no further," Honus said with a smile.

David was dumbfounded. He looked at Wagner waiting for some kind of an explanation, but the old man just stared straight into his eyes. When David put on the jersey on back in the vault, it never occurred to him that he'd be seeing Honus Wagner as an older man. He assumed that it would be like the others. If he had paid attention he would have noticed the '46 stitched inside the neck band indicating the year, and realized Wagner was a coach, not a player.

"What if I told you I walked here in the snow this afternoon to find *you?*"

"Huh?" David mumbled, confused.

"You got your puzzle piece. Now go talk to your grandpa." Honus closed his eyes and slid the little black book across the table towards David. The man who'd been tending bar approached from behind and placed his hand on David's shoulder. "It's time to go, kid."

CHAPTER 25

~~~

JIM TURNED OFF HIGHWAY 28 onto a narrow dirt road lined with trees and rusted barbed wire. On each side of the road were private property signs nearly covered by the overgrown wild grass.

"Where are we going?" David asked.

"You'll see," Jim said.

The Bronco banked to the left and David could see a bend in the road where the sun finally broke through the shady woods. Jim accelerated for a quarter of a mile before cresting above a picturesque landscape. He took his foot off the gas and coasted to a stop at flat patch surrounded by large trees.

There was a splintered picnic table that parted two aged oaks. Trees varying from green, to yellow, to orange spread out as far as the eye could see. Banks jumped out of the car and immediately began to roll on the ground like he was trying to get to an itch on his back. He was making a funny noise, almost like a growl. David laughed.

"He loves this place," Jim said.

"I can tell," David replied. "Do you come here often?"

"Not often enough. Sometimes when I want to relax and read a book I'll come here and let Banks romp around. I know the guy who owns this land. He's never here. He spends most of his time in Florida. He told me long ago to consider this place mine, and to use it whenever I wanted." Jim grabbed a basket from the back of the truck and placed it on the table. "Can you grab the ice chest, David?"

"Sure."

David placed the ice chest next to the basket. Jim removed a watermelon and a couple of ice cold Cokes. They sat across from each other and shared a picnic lunch of fried chicken and coleslaw. The afternoon escaped them while they laughed and talked about everything from girls to music to history to war. Out of nowhere David changed the subject.

"How did my dad die?"

The question fell like a lead balloon.

"You don't know?"

"Mom always said it was an accident. As I got older I just assumed it was a car accident – never really pressed her on it. Am I right?"

Jim took a deep breath through his nose while searching for the right thing to say.

"Your dad called me right after Charlie Hayes made the last out of the '96 World Series. Yankee Stadium was going nuts. It was hard to even hear him. He was yelling into the phone, *Can you hear it, Dad?* Yes, I yelled back. But he couldn't hear me. And then he said something I'll never forget. He said...*Do you remember when I sat on your shoulders when you made me watch Aaron run the bases? Do you remember that, Dad? I've been hooked ever since. I wanted to share this moment with you... love you, Dad.* I love you too, I said. But he couldn't hear me...it was too loud. And then I lost him. We had a bad connection. About twenty minutes later I was cleaning my dinner dishes when my power went out. I had no light and nothing to do so I tried calling Bill again from my cell phone. His phone rang and rang until it went to voicemail. I tried him again a few minutes later with the same result. It was odd, he always answered my calls. But I had no idea that he'd been struck by a car while stepping off a curb outside the stadium. He was rushed to New York Presbyterian hospital, but he never woke up. He was dead on arrival."

David just stared at the table. "I'm so sorry. I had no idea. I can't imagine what you must have gone through."

Jim was ashamed that David had never heard the story before. His grandson deserved better than that. He went to his car to grab an old athletic bag. He'd been saving it for the right moment. David remained at the table, stunned. Jim set the bag on the table and unzipped it. There were two baseball gloves and a ball inside. He removed one of the gloves and offered it to David.

"This was without a doubt your dad's favorite thing in the world when he was kid. He used to sleep with it! He'd have it next to him in the mornings when he'd be sitting on the couch before breakfast. He took this thing everywhere."

David put his father's glove on. The pocket was worn, stained from sweat and years in the sun.

"I want you to have it, David."

The leaves began to ruffle as a breeze blew through the trees.

"Really, you do?" David asked, smiling.

"I do."

David took his fist and pounded it into the pocket. Jim watched with a newfound sense of pride. "Would you like to play catch, David?"

"OK."

They stood and David pounded the glove some more. "Grandpa, I want to say something and I don't want you to feel like you need to respond."

"What is it?"

"I forgive you."

They spread out under the oaks and began to throw the ball back and forth, neither of them saying a word. The moment was too perfect. In the blink of an eye a generational gap was bridged. It marked the end of a long and lonely journey for Jim. For David it marked a new beginning.

CHAPTER 26

THE MOVIE THEATRE WAS IN Oneonta, about twenty miles south of Cooperstown. Jim wanted to take David to a showing of the *Pirates of the Caribbean* before going home; the simple truth to the matter is that he didn't want the day to end. The movie let out a little after nine and only a handful of people filed out past the teenage girl who swept popcorn off the stained multi-colored carpet. Jim's car was parked along the curb in front of the theatre.

"Here, catch," he said, tossing David the car keys. "You're driving us home."

"Huh?"

"You heard me."

"But I don't even have my permit."

"Look around," Jim pointed to the desolate street. "I don't think anybody's going to notice."

"But…."

"C'mon. Start it up."

Jim climbed into the passenger seat. He found this amusing, but not David who climbed in behind the wheel and stared at the dashboard.

"There's only a couple of turns between here and home. You can do it."

David started the car. The idling was intimidating.

"Go ahead and adjust the rear view mirror to your liking," Jim said.

David grabbed the mirror and pulled it down just a little bit.

"Put your foot on the break and drop it into drive," Jim instructed.

David pulled the gear lever down just as he was told.

"Now take your foot off the break and lightly step on the gas. I want you to go down to the first light and turn right. That'll take us to Highway 28."

"Are you sure about this?"

"Yep, I'm sure."

David began to pull away from the curb.

"Hold it!" Jim barked.

"What did I do wrong?"

"Do you have eyes on the back of your head?"

"No."

"Before proceeding forward you *always* need to check to see if anyone is coming up from behind. Don't just assume. Assuming gets you hurt, or worse."

David glanced over his shoulder. The coast was clear. He let out a deep breath and reluctantly stepped on the gas.

"Hey, David, just relax. You're going to do fine. By the way, if I fall asleep you know how to get home, right?"

"*What?*" David asked, flummoxed. "You can't fall asleep."

"I'm only kidding," Jim said laughing. "It's a beautiful night. Why don't you roll down the windows so we can listen to it?"

They cruised along 28 and before long David felt comfortable enough to release the vice grip he had on the steering wheel. An occasional set of headlights would emerge in the distance, and each time Jim would settle David's nerves until the car passed.

"I remember when I taught your dad how to drive. It was at night just like this. We were on the Pacific Coast Highway. I'll never forget it. We pulled up to a red light in the heart of Laguna Beach. The car next to us was full of beautiful young college-aged girls. They were all smiling at your dad trying to get his attention. He was so nervous and embarrassed he could hardly contain himself. He didn't want to look. But I sat in the passenger seat and waved at the girls, which drove your dad nuts. He was so mad at me for that."

"Oh, that's cruel."

"It was funny as hell, is what it was. How do you feel?"

"Great. It's not as hard as I thought it would be," David replied.

"Steady as she goes."

~

David was excited and went straight up stairs to call his mother in New Orleans. Jim stepped onto the deck with his laptop in one hand and cell phone in the other. He sat at the table and watched Banks who stood at the edge of the deck with his nose through the railing, smelling something below. His old friend was starting to show his age. He was slower and becoming hard of hearing, and his once golden muzzle was growing grayer by the day.

Jim knew at some point in the coming days he'd have to tell David about the cancer. He never anticipated growing attached to the boy he'd abandoned long ago. The thought of telling him pained him more than the disease ever could. He started to think about time, how it's measured, and how unappreciated it can be. If only he could have more of it. Like one more day with Catherine; a simple walk on the beach. If only he could have more day with Bill; a day game in the bleachers. If only David could stay longer and experience a Cooperstown winter. If only he had made better use of his time when it really mattered most. His train of thought was interrupted by the ringing of his phone. The caller ID said MARTHA. He pushed the button to answer. "What are you doing up so late?" he asked.

"I hope I didn't wake you," Martha replied.

"You didn't. I'm just out on my deck getting ready to write a little."

"I've got some great news," Martha replied.

"I could use some right about now."

"You promise not to get mad?"

"If it's great why would I get mad? I'm not sure I like where this is going, but go on."

"I have a good friend from college whose best friends with a high profile literary agent in the city. I asked if she could take the pages of your manuscript and somehow get them to the agent. It didn't take her long. I just got a call from my friend, and the agent loves it. She thinks it's a fantastic concept and wants more."

"More? Are you serious?"

"I'm serious. I'm sorry, Jim. I should have told you. You know I'm your biggest fan. I wanted to help but I didn't want to say anything in case it fell through. I didn't want to get your hopes up. The agent wants to contact you and talk about a possible book deal."

Jim fixated on a crack between planks in the wood deck.

"Are you mad, Jim?"

"No, Martha, I'm not mad," Jim said. "I'm lost for words. I was just sitting out here alone thinking about *time* and what a precious commodity it is. I'm just thankful I had time to get this done."

"You're going to get a phone call tomorrow. The agents name is Stella Weiss. She's going to want to set up a meeting with you once the book is complete."

"I'm just about there, Martha."

"Good. I'm so happy you found this story. It was in you all along! I know how much you were struggling with the original concept you had."

"This never would have happened had it not been for David. He made me see things differently."

"He's going to love it, Jim."

"I hope so…I really hope so."

"Get back to writing. I'm really proud of you, Jim."

"You're a great friend, Martha. Thank you."

Jim hung up the phone and watched the screen go black just like the light in David's window. The pain in his stomach suddenly spiked, but he had become accustomed to it. He opened his laptop and began to pour his thoughts onto a blank Word document. This took his mind off the pain more than any prescription could. The words flowed on the page like the tears he wanted to cry. The end became more and more apparent.

And the manuscript was almost done, too.

CHAPTER 27

David's eyes opened wide from a dead sleep. He sprung out of bed, his breathing heavy. He checked the clock, 11:28 PM. Time was on his side. He got dressed and rushed downstairs. Banks was sleeping in the study; startled by the sudden commotion. When he jumped up, his collar rattled causing David to stop in his tracks.

"*Shhhh.*" He patted Banks on the head, "Good boy."

He collected his thoughts before walking outside; what he was about to attempt could change everything. He closed the front door quietly and glanced at the garage where he had left the bicycle against the side wall. The crickets were loud against the quiet night. He hopped on the bicycle and set out under a blanket of stars. Within minutes his heart and mind raced against each other, and he didn't stop pedaling until he reached the steps of the Hall of Fame.

He leaned the bike against shrubs on the left side of the museum and climbed the small steps. A police car turned onto Pioneer Street a block away giving David pause. He checked over his shoulder one last time before inserting the key that he'd taken off of Jim's key ring. Once inside, he disarmed the alarm by entering the memorized code.

The coast was clear.

He took the elevator down straight for the vault. His hands trembled when he swiped the card over the security pad. Nothing happened. He swiped it again. And again.

"Damn it. Don't do this to me, now," he yelled.

He pulled on the handle and began slapping his hand on the door out of frustration.

"Well, well. Aren't *you* frustrated?"

The voice made David cringe. He turned. Michael stood next to him.

"What are *you* doing here?" David asked.

"Umm, you're the one who should be answering that question. I work here, remember? But what are *you* doing here and how'd you get in? Isn't this breaking and entering? I believe I could have you arrested. This isn't going to be good for you and your grandpa, I can assure you that."

"C'mon, you don't have to do...."

"This isn't going to be good for *you* unless you take a hike," a third voice chimed in.

David and Michael turned. Walking down the hall towards them with his newsboy cap in hand was Arthur Page. David looked shocked, like he had seen a ghost. Michael just looked confused.

"Who are *you*?" Michael asked.

Arthur didn't answer.

"OK, let me try this again. *Who* are you?"

"Are you writing a book?" Arthur replied.

"Maybe," Michael replied with overt sarcasm.

"Well, leave out a page and make it a mystery. The kid is down here because he asked me to help him on a project he's doing for his grandpa before he leaves to go back home. This is the only time he can do it without his grandpa finding out. And let me fill you in on a little something else. You don't know me or who I know around here. So, I suggest you march on outta' here before you find yourself in a position you don't want to be in. And not a word about this to anybody, you understand?"

"Yes sir," Michael replied.

Michael took off down the hallway and didn't look back.

"Wow, that was close," David said letting out a heavy sigh of relief. "Why'd you do that for me? Who are you anyway?"

Arthur ignored the question. "I know why you're here tonight kid."

"Why?"

"You were gonna try to go back in time and save your father. Weren't you?"

"How'd you know that?"

"C'mon. Let's go for a walk."

David's adrenaline flushed away like a fading tide. He didn't have the strength to protest. And for some strange reason he felt at ease, like everything was going to be OK. They walked back to the elevator without another word spoken, taking it to the main lobby, and out the front door where they sat on a bench in a courtyard. It was off the beaten path where nobody would see them at this time of night.

"How'd you know why I was here?" David asked.

"I'm like a leprechaun, kid. Remember?"

"Who are you? Tell me."

Arthur ignored the question, again.

"How come the vault wouldn't open?" David asked, still frustrated.

"Because you were going to try to change history. And you can't do that."

"Why not?"

"Because that changes everything. Besides, that's not why you were picked."

"Picked?"

"Yes. To go back in time."

"You mean *you* had something to do with that?"

"Do you think it just *happened*?"

"Why me?"

"It has everything to do with your grandpa."

"Grandpa?"

"That's right."

"What does he have to do with this?"

"Because I needed somebody to help me."

"Help you?"

"I'm sorry to be the one who has to tell you this. Your grandpa is sick, kid."

"He's sick? What are you talking about? How would you know? When I told him about you that day we met by the lake he had no idea who you were."

"That's because he doesn't, though we have interacted. Sometimes I have to go through others to get to the ones I want. And in doing so I often open their eyes up to possibilities they would have never have known otherwise."

"Who are you, some sort of baseball God?"

"I am the keeper of baseball's past. I oversee an extensive library of games. Every game ever played, as a matter of fact. They're all catalogued and at any given time can be replayed in their exact form. Not just the games either, but every fan, every hot dog vendor, anything associated with a particular game. It's all there. Even the road trips, train rides and hotel bars. I'm the guy who can give it all back. There are a lot of old timers who want to relive a spectacular moment or a great play they made, hell, even a fling on the road. It keeps me really busy. Where I come from, anything connected to baseball's past becomes present to the beholder. *Anything!* So you might imagine I'm pretty popular with some of the old guys when they come home to greener pastures."

"You mean when they die?"

"That's right, kid. My name is Arthur Page. And yes, I am the baseball God."

"I don't believe you," David replied, defiant.

"OK then, let me ask you something. Do you think it's normal to toss on an old jersey and travel back in time? How do you suppose that happened? And once you were there, who do you think sent you back to the present every time?

"So *you* were the one on the train and in the clubhouse? And it was you that took the photo of me in Washington!"

"I was the one in the bar with Honus, too. Now do you believe me?"

"Yes," David replied sheepishly.

"I guess you could say I'm kind of like a scout. Aside from my duties of watching over every game ever played, I go around and recruit those who deserve a chance to have baseball live forever within them."

"What do you mean by recruit?"

"Your grandpa has paid his dues in life and then some. He's been through a lot. But he's also made a significant mistake in his life by turning his back on you and he knows it. But I believe he's doing what he can right now to make things right. And I believe in redemption. He's exactly the kind of person I look for, somebody who'll appreciate what I have to offer. I can make your grandpa a happy man forever. So are you ready to listen?"

"Yes."

"Good. I need a favor from you, kid. I need you to tell your grandpa about your secret of going back in time. It's the key that'll unlock his biggest question in life, once and for all."

"You mean the baseball?"

"Yes."

"Mr. Page, is there a baseball heaven?"

"Look around you…we're in it right now."

"You mean Cooperstown?"

"Ever heard of heaven on earth?"

Arthur began to walk away. He stopped and looked back. "Please tell him," he said. "Time is running out. If anyone can do it, it's you."

He turned the corner and was erased by the night.

David remained seated, motionless. It all made sense now.

CHAPTER 28

~

CATHERINE'S PRESENCE WAS SORELY MISSED inside the small waiting room at the hospital. She would've had a way to calm Jim's nerves; something the three cups of stale coffee exacerbated. She'd only been gone a few months, and Jim was doing everything he could to keep himself together. The arrival of his first grandchild gave him hope, like a dry rung on an otherwise slippery ladder. It would give him and Bill something to focus on, something to love together in an attempt to carry on without the single greatest woman either of them had ever known.

Susie's parents lived on the east coast and couldn't make it out in time for the birth that came two weeks early. And but for an occasional nurse passing through in royal blue scrubs, the room was empty leaving Jim by himself as it approached midnight.

He had it all planned out. If it was a girl, he was going to spoil her with flowers and dresses and all things sweet. He was going to take walks in the park with her during the day and read her princess stories at night. If it was a boy, he was going to continue the Danly tradition of baseball and hope that maybe someday he'd be watching him on the manicured infields of major league diamonds across the country. But life comes without blueprints, and plans are often swept away by fate. Never could he imagine running away from the child all together. But never did he imagine the living hell he'd be faced with in only two months' time, a hell so bad that with the evil influence of booze he contemplated the ultimate bail out.

When Bill pushed open the double doors, Jim stood and took a deep breath. The news of a healthy baby boy brought them together in the middle of the room where their embrace was met with tears of joy.

Jim cupped both hands around his coffee mug and watched the steam rise in front of his face. The lake always looked like glass in the early mornings, so calming. He'd give anything for a second chance. Not because of his worsening condition, but to redeem his unmitigated failures as a grandfather. If all else failed, which up until now it had, he hoped the time spent with David, along with the book, would be seen as a pardon in his only grandchild's eyes.

The sound of the screen door sliding open snapped Jim out of his daydream. "Good morning," David said.

"Morning," Jim replied without taking his eyes off the lake. "You're up earlier than usual, aren't you?"

"Couldn't sleep anymore."

"Well, there's some orange juice in the fridge. Why don't you grab a glass and come join me?"

"OK."

David helped himself to a glass of orange juice and returned to the deck. He pulled up a chair next to Jim and the two sat silent underneath the still morning sky. The silence became deafening until David finally spoke out.

"Are you sick?"

Jim took a long sip from his steaming hot coffee mug. He paused. "I was going to tell you."

"What is it?"

"Stomach cancer," Jim replied without taking his eyes off the lake.

"How bad?"

"It's bad, David. How'd you know?"

"I just put it all together. When I first got here you seemed thinner than what I remembered. I've noticed you wince a couple of times over simple things, and something just didn't seem right. Were you ever going to tell me?"

"Two weeks ago it didn't matter. Your mother would have been notified, and she presumably would have told you and that would have been it. But things changed once you arrived. And I'm so thankful for that. I've been spending a lot of time thinking about how I was going to tell you. To be honest, I've been dreading it."

"You can beat it, right? You're doing everything possible aren't you?"

"I watched your grandmother suffer when she was taking chemo and other drugs. They all made her even more sick. I vowed never to do that to myself."

"So what do we do now?"

There was something so innocent about David's question that it brought a smile to Jim's face.

"Look David, I was told three years ago that I had six months to live. So what do we do? We get up every day and open the blinds because we can't run from life, besides there's a lot to see out there. We read books and continue to grow our minds. We try to find simple pleasures, whatever they may be because there are no guarantees. All we can do is take it in stride, and take life one day at a time. And no matter how much the deck is stacked against you, you never quit."

"It doesn't seem fair," David said with a look of despair.

"Who said life was fair? You know better than that. Listen, regardless of what happens I want you to remember something that'll serve you well in life. And that's to learn how to accept losses without being defeated."

David shook his head. He was despondent and Jim knew it.

"Well I think today's the day," Jim said.

"Huh?"

"Get dressed. We're going to get some breakfast and take the boat out." Jim stood and patted David's head. He walked inside and headed upstairs while David remained in the chair with a pensive gaze.

Yes, he thought. *Today is the day.*

CHAPTER 29

THE BLUE AND WHITE BOAT glided over the water leaving
a long trail of whitewash in its wake. A sense of freedom
liberated David from the dubious thoughts of Jim's cancer
and the notion of divulging his secret. Jim stood close while
David steered the boat towards the scenic horizon book-
ended by trees. Their smiles were as wide as the sky over
Cooperstown; neither wanting the moment to end.

"What's that up there?" David shouted, trying to penetrate the wind and roar of the inboard engine.

"That's Kingfisher tower," Jim yelled. "Keep going and
pull back on the throttle when you get a little closer."

The castle was made out of gray rocks, and it stood
about sixty feet high. It looked straight out of the Middle
Ages; the only thing missing was knights on horseback. He
eased back on the throttle bringing the boat to a gradual
stop.

"Go ahead, put it in neutral, and shut it off," Jim said. David turned the boat off and within a minute or two the water around them turned to glass.

"The tower was built in 1876 by Edward Clark. He was one of the founders of the Singer Sewing Machine Company. He made a fortune in real estate investments. Clark's grandson, Stephen, founded the Baseball Hall of Fame and Stephen's granddaughter is Jane Forbes Clark."

"Who's that?"

"The chairman of the board of directors of Hall of Fame."

"Your boss?"

"You could say that, yes."

"It's so mystical looking."

"They say that Clark built the tower to *beautify* the lake. Sometimes I think he built it to give the baseball God a place to live."

David looked stunned.

"I'm only kidding, David."

"Yeah, but do you believe in that kind of stuff?" David asked.

"Only when I see the unimaginable happen on a baseball field. Then it makes me wonder."

"What if I told you there was one?"

"One what?"

"A baseball God."

"What are you talking about?" Jim asked.

"Grandpa, I've been holding onto a secret since the second day I was here. I wanted to tell you the day we went to Wrigley Field, but I didn't know how."

"Tell me what?"

"That first night when I was at the Hall and you told me to take a walk. I was up on the second floor when an elevator door opened. Nobody got off so I stepped in. I pressed the down button, and when it stopped I got off."

"In the basement?"

"I started walking and noticed a card lying on the ground. When I picked it up I realized that it was some sort of access card."

"To the vault!"

"Yes."

"Continue."

"I waved the card over the black pad on the wall and the door opened. I was amazed with all the stuff inside. When I saw the box that said Mathewson on it I took it down. Do you remember when I asked you if you ever tried on jerseys?"

"Yes, go on."

"I put his jersey on."

"You didn't!"

"Something unexplainable happened. I blacked out and the next thing I knew I was on an old train at night. There was a man in the back of the car by himself. I walked back to him and he introduced himself to me as Christy Mathewson."

"OK, enough of this nonsense."

"It's not nonsense," David argued.

"David, please."

David removed his black book from his pocket. His frustration mounted and he began to wave the notebook in front of Jim. "Then how do you think I got these?" He handed the small book over to Jim. "Go on, open it. Take a look at the first page," he said, almost defiant.

Jim took the book from David's hand. He inspected the first page, and though he didn't want to admit it, he was stumped. Throughout the years working at the Hall of Fame, he had spent hours with some of the most respected authenticators in the country on everything from under-garments to signatures. He had developed a trained eye, learned the various nuances of signatures, and how to tell which ones were real and which ones weren't. He stared at the names in the book and knew beyond all doubt that they were real.

"Where'd you get this?" Jim asked, perplexed.

"He gave it to me?"

"*Who* did?"

"Christy Mathewson."

"Stop it, David. Where'd you get it?"

"I told you."

"*Damn it*, David."

The emotions began to crash down on David all at once.

The cancer.

The secret.

Going home.

He turned his back to Jim and stared out towards Kingfisher Tower. And in this moment of transition from boy to man, he had to fight with everything he had not to show his emotions. "I have lied awake at night many times thinking about how I was going to explain it all to you. I knew I couldn't leave here without telling you, but I didn't want to risk ruining the progress we've made either. When you took me through the gallery and showed me the First Class, I took your words to heart. I wanted to learn more about them. I know I shouldn't have tried on the Mathewson jersey, but I couldn't resist. It's like it called my name. And when I experienced the unbelievable, I had to go back and try it again."

Jim scanned the page once again wanting to find flaws in the signatures. But Mathewson's name was written to perfection just as it always was. So was Johnson's. The Wagner signature almost had the appearance of a right handed person using their left hand to write, and Cobb's had his trademark swoosh as an extension of the last B underlining his entire name with small quote marks in the center.

"I don't believe it," he whispered. "But the signatures... *they're real!*"

"You've got to believe me," David pleaded. "I've met the four Hall of Famers in that book, the entire First Class except one."

"*Ruth.*" Jim observed.

"That's right," David affirmed. "Do you remember my first morning here when I went for a walk along the lake's edge and I ran into that old guy who seemed to know you? Well his name is Arthur Page and he's...."

"*Arthur Page?*" Jim snapped.

It all came back to him: Camilli's steakhouse and the note on the cocktail napkin with the reference to *Knucks*. "Do you *know* him?" Jim asked.

David didn't answer. He continued to stare at Kingfisher Tower.

"Do you?" Jim asked again.

"*He's* the baseball God."

"David, stop."

"I know how much that ball means to you, and how much it's tearing you up inside. One way or another, you need to find out. You need validation. I haven't gone back to see Ruth on purpose because I want you to go."

"Go?"

"Back in time! I want you to try. Please. You owe it to yourself to try."

"I think we ought to head back now. What do you say?"

"I know this all sounds so crazy. But I would never lie to you. Never in a million years would I."

"I don't think you would, David. But this is all a bit much to comprehend right now. C'mon, let's go back."

Jim started the engine and pushed the throttle down. The water churned like the emotions running through David's mind. He stared at the tree lined hills as they headed back, until his eyes went out of focus and everything was a green blur. He wondered if he'd made a huge mistake. He wondered if things would ever be the same between the two of them. But he had to do it because Arthur Page asked him to. Now it was up to Jim to find out for himself.

CHAPTER 30

~

DAVID TUCKED THE BLACK AND white photo into a folder. He zipped his suitcase and checked the view from the window one last time in an effort to sear it into his memory. He could hear the ticking of the grandfather clock downstairs. He hadn't noticed it since the day he arrived, but now it seemed louder than ever because it was counting down the seconds before he had to leave it all behind. He proceeded to walk downstairs without waking Jim and grabbed a glazed donut before stepping outside.

As he walked along the trail on the lakes edge the magic of Cooperstown never seemed so undeniable; the colors of blue and green so vibrant and boundless. It was hard to comprehend that he'd wake up tomorrow on the other side of the country and his normal life, whatever that was, would resume right where it left off. He'd be hanging with his friends, soon school would start, and this sleepy town where legends live would begin to vanish in his mind.

David took a seat on the bench and stretched his feet in front of him. He clasped his hands together and placed them behind his head. He heard what sounded like footsteps coming from behind.

"I had a feeling I'd find you out here," Jim said.

"It's amazing. I don't want to leave it."

"It'll always be here for you."

While David knew that to be true, he also knew that his grandfather *wouldn't* be. He didn't want to think about that. His bags were packed, and he looked forward to seeing his mother, but a big part of him wanted to stay in Cooperstown and continue to live this paranormal life. Jim took a seat next to David on the bench.

"I couldn't sleep last night."

"Me either," David replied.

"I'm sorry about yesterday."

"You don't have to be sorry. I understand. But I couldn't leave here without telling you. Whether or not you choose to believe it is up to you."

"I'm happy we had this chance to be together, David. I never thought I'd get this opportunity. I didn't deserve it."

"I'm glad, too," David replied. "This is so hard, though. I'm leaving knowing that I'll probably never see you again."

"Stranger things have happened, right?" Jim said with a touch of sarcasm.

They laughed.

"I'll make you deal," Jim said. "I'll try to make it out for your birthday."

"Really?"

"I said I'll try. It'll all depend on how I'm feeling."

"Will you promise me one thing?" David asked.

"Sure."

"At least consider what I told you yesterday."

Jim acquiesced. "OK. I'll consider it."

Jim looked at this watch. "C'mon, we've got to get going."

~

Jim dropped David off at the airport in Syracuse. They walked up to the security check-point and hugged one another, neither wanting to let go. Jim patted David on the cheek.

"I love you, David."

"I know."

They parted ways and soon David blended in with the crowd of people on the other side of security until he disappeared. Jim drove back to Cooperstown in complete silence; at times wiping away tears of joy and sorrow. He thought about the gains they'd made and the lost years never to be restored. David's visit taught Jim you can never run from loss, that in the end everything comes full circle and inevitably catches up to you.

He wasn't ready to go back to an empty house so he opted for Camilli's where he pushed himself up against the bar. He glossed over a dinner menu. Glenn greeted him with a smile and a stiff drink, not his usual glass of red wine. He could see the sadness in Jim's eyes; knew he'd need somebody to listen. Over the next several hours Jim spoke about David and what a fine young man he was, and how he cherished the days he spent with him and longed for more. He talked about his book in great detail, and what it meant to him to finish it now more than ever. And he confessed to Glenn that he was dying. It was the first time Jim had mentioned it to anybody other than Martha and Stan. The news rendered Glenn speechless. When the night drew to an end the two hugged at the edge of the bar, and Jim reassured Glenn not to worry; that he'd be back again, and again.

Jim parked his car on his driveway and stood outside in the pitch dark listening to the crickets occupy the night. When he walked inside he was greeted by Banks who seemed too tired earlier in the day to come along. It was another impending sign that the years were catching up to his most loyal pal. He didn't want to think about that – not on this night. He placed his keys on the kitchen counter, grabbed a bottle of scotch from his mini bar, and poured himself a glass. On his way out of the kitchen he noticed a folder on the table. He opened it. Inside was the photo of Walter Johnson that David had confiscated from the research center. There was a yellow Post-it note that read *please believe me* on it. He peeled the paper off the photo exposing an implausible truth. Those eyes were all too familiar, captured somewhere far away in another place, in another time.

"Oh my," he whispered.

He dropped the photo on the table and stepped outside onto the deck. Fall began to catch up to summer, evident by the slight chill in the air. He leaned against the wood railing to extol the lake that spread out before him under the glow of the moon. And then he saw something most unusual.

Perhaps he was tired.

Maybe he had too much to drink.

He had to strain to focus on the object near the center of the lake. The night was strangely quiet and he could hear the subtle splashes of what sounded like oars hitting the water. He watched as a row boat drifted through the moon's brilliance. A man in the boat rested his oars and waved jubilantly at Jim before continuing into the darkness and out of sight. A rush of cool air passed through Jim and his spirits were lifted. He waved back to the faceless man who was now gone and then he retired for the night. Tomorrow was a new day. Jim Danly would never let another one go to waste.

SIX MONTHS LATER

A LIGHT SNOW FELL, GIVING Cooperstown a reprieve from the wrath it had endured for three straight days. Jim walked to his office, but stopped along the way to peek out the large windows that overlooked the courtyard. The statues of Johnny Podres and Roy Campanella were covered in fresh powder, and the glow of the moon reflected off the snowpack. The stores and restaurants were all barren, Main Street was empty, and the roads leading into town were all closed making it impossible for the most dedicated tourists to visit.

He entered his office and sat behind his desk. It hadn't been this clean since his first day working there. The only items on it were the case with the baseball inside and an advanced copy of his book titled: *A Fan's Memoir – A Gift for a Grandson*. The release date was set for Opening Day; whether he'd be around to sign any copies was another story.

The last few weeks had been hell on Jim. His health had taken a turn for the worse, and he lost Banks to a tumor that was discovered too late. He picked up the book, held it with both hands, and stared at the cover. It was a close-up picture of the called shot baseball resting atop the splintered picnic table between the two oaks where he and David enjoyed a brilliant afternoon.

It had been six months since David left and Jim missed him terribly. He hadn't let two days go by without talking to his grandson; quite a contrast from the old Jim Danly. His health got in the way of keeping his promise about visiting David on his birthday. But he was grateful for the time he shared with him and the subsequent bond they developed. It was in these quiet moments of reflection that Jim would think about mortality. He would also think about David's stories of the flannel past and wonder, what if?

A tear fell onto his desk, then another. He smeared them away with the palm of his hand, and then he grabbed a small box from his credenza full of Styrofoam popcorn. He opened the top drawer to his desk and removed a blank index card and inscribed the following words: *Because of you I found my voice. Use your passion and find yours.* He placed the card inside the front cover of his memoir and put it at the bottom of the box.

Then came the easy part!

After forty-eight years of agonizing over that damn baseball, Jim picked up the case and removed the ball. He lifted the ball up to his nose and drew in one last deep breath with his eyes closed. A slight smile formed and everything was OK. He placed the ball inside the box and packed it in with Styrofoam before taping it shut. He addressed the box to *Mr. David Danly* and placed it on Martha's desk with the following instructions written on another index card: *Please send this for me. If David calls tell him I went in search of flannel. He'll understand.* He dropped the plastic ball case in the trash, closed the door to the office behind him, and turned out the lights to the research center for the last time.

He couldn't get David out of his mind as he walked through the museum, passed the bookstore, through the library atrium, down the ramp with the famous documents, into the plaque gallery, and up inductee row where he finally stopped at the elevator doors. He pushed the down button and waited. The door opened and he stepped inside where a series of random thoughts washed over him. His heart raced like wind over a raging fire until he discerned a voice he hadn't heard in years calm his nerves. It was his father calling him home just like he used to when the sun dipped below the rooftops in the old neighborhood. Knucks would stand on the front porch with the *Chicago Tribune* rolled up to his mouth. And in a deep voice, pretending to be the public address announcer at Wrigley Field, he'd yell, *"Now batting for the Cubs, Jim Danly. Time to come home, Jimmy."* The kids on the street would get a kick out it, wishing their fathers would call them home in the same fashion. The voice inside Jim's head never sounded clearer.

The elevator doors opened and his father's voice disappeared. He wanted it back so badly. He'd walked these halls towards the vault too many times to count, but always for someone else. Now it was for him, and he felt like a kid inside. The game of baseball will do that to you if you let it.

He waved his access card over the pad and opened the heavy door. Without hesitating, he walked the narrow path under the cool vault air. In a room with over 35,000 artifacts he knew precisely what he was looking for and where it was. He stopped and looked up to his left and found the box with RUTH in the lower left corner. He pulled it down and removed the lid. Inside was a gray flannel jersey folded in half with navy blue block letters across the front spelling NEW YORK. In the back of the collar, embroidered in red chain-stitch was *Ruth '32*. He unbuttoned the jersey and began to laugh out loud. He slipped his arms inside and within seconds his father's voice appeared again, calling him home one more time. And then there was Catherine's voice with inaudible words and laughter all rolled into one. The sounds were intimate and free, and warmed him to his core. He became dizzy and took a seat on a plastic chair in the middle of the room and closed his eyes.

"…Dad…Dad, over here."

"*Bill?*" Jim whispered. "Come to me, Billy."

~⟋

It was cold and the sky had a grayish tint. Red, white and blue bunting draped from the exterior of the stadium as far as the eye could see. Uniformed policeman on horseback kept the peace between the seas of people surrounding Wrigley Field. Shiny black Model-T Fords tried to make their way through the crowd like salmon swimming upstream. The men all wore wool overcoats with fedoras and pungent cigar smoke blanketed the air. Hot peanuts were for sale, scorecards too. Jim walked along the first base side of the ballpark, parallel to West Addison Street. He stopped to buy a scorecard. The thin booklet read: 1932 World Series. New York Yankees vs. Chicago Cubs, Game 3, 1:15 PM.

"Do you know what inning they're in?" Jim asked the vendor.

"Going to the top of five," he answered.

This is it, he thought.

He had to make his way towards Sheffield Avenue. He knew Ruth was up second behind Joe Sewell who'd ground-out to shortstop. Jim's pace became fast, almost frantic, trying to weave in and out of the crowd. If there were 49,000 people inside the stadium it felt like that many outside, maybe more. But when he turned the corner everything changed. The street was empty and quiet.

He looked up at the American Flag in center field. It was blowing straight out like it was pulled by a string.

The placid surroundings were interrupted by a thunderous roar from inside the stadium. Jim's eyes were fixated on the flag when he noticed a lone ball fly right through his sights. The ball smacked the middle of the street and rolled a good fifty feet before coming to a stop against the curb in front of a coffee shop. He stood still, never taking his eyes off the ball. The crowd eventually hushed and he began to walk towards the ball, but stopped when a man wearing a navy blue three-piece suit stepped outside the coffee shop to pick it up. The man's head was down with a fedora pulled low making it hard to see his face. One thing was certain – it was not his father. He didn't want to believe what he was seeing. His mind harkened back to his Mother's voice, *"Your father wanted you to have this…your father wanted you to have this."* He felt sick to his stomach.

She lied.

What started off as a faint rumble quickly became a loud stampede of teenagers running wild down Sheffield Avenue. There must have been a dozen of them, all hollering at the top of their lungs.

"Hey, give me that ball," a boy yelled.

Another one quipped, "That's my ball, Mister."

The man in the three-piece suit was walking back towards the coffee shop when he stopped with his back towards Jim, waiting for the boys who closed in. Within seconds they had him surrounded like a pack of wolves with their hands extended, pleading for the ball.

"That's mine," a boy yelled.

"No it's not, it's mine," another one demanded.

But there was one boy standing in the back of the bunch not saying a word. The man spotted him and handed the ball over to him, rewarding him for his polite disposition. The other boys ran off in protest leaving the boy with the ball alone with the man in the suit. Their backs were to Jim who watched with great interest from across the street.

"Where did you come from, Mister?" the boy asked.

"Oh I come and go," the man said. "I'm like a leprechaun, kid."

Leprechaun?

Jim froze.

"You hang on to that ball, you here?" The man said. "It's a special one."

"Thanks a lot, mister. " The happy boy turned and began to run back down the street towards his dejected friends. Jim got a clear look at the boy's face as he ran by. His dirty blonde bangs hung over his forehead; a smile from ear to ear. And there was an unforgettable twinkle in his familiar blue eyes.

"Dad," he tried to call out. But the word seemed too heavy, unable to be heard.

And then he began to cry.

The boy continued down Sheffield Avenue without noticing Jim, who was now sobbing on the sidewalk. The man in the three-piece suit crossed the street.

"Hi, Jim."

Jim stared at the man for what seemed like a minute before he could even utter a word.

"It's you.....Arthur," Jim said.

He smiled. "That's right, Jim."

"What's happening?"

"Well, I'd say you just witnessed something special."

"She was right," Jim said while trying to gain his composure.

"Of course she was. That'll teach you never to doubt your mother again." Arthur said with a smile.

"Where are we?"

"You tell me."

Jim looked behind. Wrigley Field had disappeared into a vast sea of white nothingness that stretched out forever. His feet were still planted firmly on Sheffield Avenue. That he was sure of. The coffee shop was still in front of him across the street.

"Is this heaven?"

"What are you feeling right now, Jim?"

"It's hard to explain. It's an overwhelming feeling of love. It's beyond words how strong it is."

Arthur smiled. He took out a cigarette and lit it.

"You know, Jim, sometimes I have to go through others to get to the ones I want. In doing so, I open their eyes up to possibilities they would have never known otherwise known."

"You mean David?"

"That's right." Arthur took a long drag on his cigarette. "He's a good kid, Jim."

"Yes, he is."

"He's going to be OK."

"Are you sure?"

"I wouldn't lie to you."

"But what if I want to go back?"

"Are you sure you want to?" Arthur said motioning towards the coffee shop across the street. Jim looked inside and saw a handsome young man sitting at a table behind the window reading a book and drinking a cup of coffee, oblivious.

"Oh my...." Jim whimpered, unable to finish the thought. Arthur offered him a handkerchief.

"You can stay here, Jim."

"Stay here?"

Arthur didn't answer.

"You mean....die?"

"I can tie up all the loose ends back in Cooperstown. That won't be a problem at all. Your friends at the museum, they know you're sick. I'll tell them that you passed away, and I was sent to handle all the arrangements."

"But what about David?"

"He'll be fine. Trust me."

"Can I ask you something? Why did you write that note about my dad on the napkin at Camilli's that night?"

"Because I wanted you to start thinking about *what if*."

"Is he here, too?"

"Your dad?"

"Yes."

"Everyone you love is here, Jim. And they're all waiting."

"Catherine, too?"

"Everyone."

"Can I go see my son?"

"I was wondering when you were going to ask."

They began to cross the street towards eternity. And with each passing step the street behind them turned into a soft white liquid that faded like ripples in a pool. As they approached the coffee shop, Jim and Bill made eye contact for the first time. All the years of heartbreak seemed like a fleeting moment. Jim stopped and stared, nervous to reunite with his only child. From behind the window Bill smiled like he'd been waiting for his dad all along. "Hi, Dad" he mouthed. Jim smiled as a tear rolled off his cheek. Arthur and Jim began walking simultaneously towards the front door when Arthur paused and fanned his arm out with an open hand and said, "After you, Jim."

AFTERWARD

~

July 23, 2062

DAVID LOOKED AT HIS WATCH; it was half past four in the afternoon. He must have dozed. He hadn't slept much the night before; they didn't get back from the gala until almost midnight. His nerves kept him up a good three hours longer. The lake was alive with white sails taut by a strong breeze blowing from the west. He would often see the lake in his dreams and think about the afternoon he spent with his grandpa. And how he wanted to do it again – with his grandkids. Perhaps tomorrow. Right now he needed to get back to the Otesaga, the historic hotel on the banks of Otsego Lake, so he could clean up for dinner with his wife, Maddie, and their extended family, all waiting for him.

Fifty years had gone by like pages in a flip book. He had three daughters and seven grandchildren whom he loved more than anything. The road he traveled to get here today wasn't always smooth. It had come with a lot of hard work, time away from his family along with turmoil, lost friendships, and even threats.

When David returned home from his visit with his grandpa all those summers ago, he tried to get back to a normal life. When the box arrived with the baseball and memoir inside, it stoked a flame that still burned like a pilot. He read his grandpa's memoir from cover to cover, and then read it again. He read everything he could get his hands on and finished high school at the top of his class. Then there was the baseball. He would have traded it in a heartbeat for more time with his grandpa. The ball really didn't mean that much to him, only that his grandpa wanted him to have it. It was his *grandpa's* struggle, not his. Besides, after all of the years gone by, there wasn't a person around who'd accept his story and the saga would continue. But in some curious way he found strength in the baseball and used it as a subliminal metaphor of sorts for things deemed impossible. It inspired him to leave no stone unturned, to do whatever it took to get answers – a discipline that would serve him well in life.

He took up writing for pleasure and honed his craft all the way through college until he graduated from the University of Southern California with a degree in journalism. That's when he began writing for a local newspaper covering the Los Angeles Angels, and before long, his little black notebook was full of tidbits and anecdotes from the stars of the day. He never forgot Bernard Kastner's words of wisdom: *Love, Listen & Trust.* Within a few years he gained the respect of not only the home town team, but the visiting clubs too.

He teamed up with an artist friend from college who'd sketch players like the vintage sports cartoonists from the 1930's and 40's. The columns and the cartoons became an overnight success, which led to a bi-weekly column picked up by the AP called *Danly's Dirt.* His columns gained him national recognition. After fifteen years he moved onto MLB.com where he not only continued to write, but also picked up his own weekly cable show that provided intellect and commentaries on the business of baseball.

By 2035 David was almost forty and considered the most proficient baseball writer in the country. This was also the time when he knocked the baseball world on its backside with a Pulitzer Prize winning book titled *Basefall: America's National Travesty.* He exposed a nefarious underworld of designer drugs and racketeering linked to Major League Baseball, which led to subsequent investigations resulting in the indictment of two club owners, multiple general managers, as well as several big name players. Never before had the game been so shamed and in such peril. Fans left in droves, and they weren't coming back.

The heroic whistleblower in the book was the power hitting first baseman for the Cincinnati Reds named Stro Snider. He gave David the inside scoop on everything. For

David, it was a treasure trove of information. For Snider, it was a huge risk, but one he felt compelled to take. Snider was thirty and a four time MVP. He'd gone four straight seasons with fifty or more home runs. In 2034 he shattered Hack Wilson's single season RBI record with an astonishing 201. Snider was a farm boy who kept his hair above his ears and was clean shaven for every game. He never used batting gloves and wore a coat and tie when the club travelled, even though his teammates didn't. He'd sign autographs until every last kid got theirs. He refused to cover his body with ink, which seemed to be a prerequisite for being a big leaguer. He was as clean as they come, and a true twentieth century throwback if there ever was one.

On the day the book was published, Snider held a press conference that many felt saved baseball. For too long he was accused of using performance enhancing drugs, while players he knew *were* users got off scot free. The writers called him a modern day Jackie Robinson for having the courage to stand up and name names. He condemned the players union for knowingly protecting dirty players while clean ones were forced to live under clouds of suspicion. He urged clean players in the game to break the union and follow him. Before long players came out of the shadows to cross the line, while some pretty big names fell by the wayside into baseball purgatory.

In Danly's consequential book he created a concept for a new kind of baseball commissioner – a commissioner by committee. He felt it would be in baseball's best interest to eliminate a lone commissioner beholden to the owners and thus susceptible to corruption. Instead he suggested replacing it with a majority rule system with a panel of five: a former player and umpire, a writer, broadcaster and a retired baseball executive. The idea garnered the attention of many around the game and quickly gained traction. With a few minor tweaks it was enacted in the winter of 2037. Danly's writing peers unanimously threw in their support for him to be on that panel where he remained for twenty years.

The game was back and bigger than ever.

Stro Snider retired a few years after his historic press conference because of an ailing back and two bad knees. In his career he racked up 539 home runs and drove in 1,991 runs. He went home to his farm to breed race horses, started a beef business, and rarely participated in anything pertaining to baseball. He was inducted to the Baseball Hall of Fame in 2045.

And now on this brilliant blue July afternoon almost twenty years later it was David's turn. After writing about the game for almost four decades, winning a Pulitzer Prize, and spearheading a new commissioner's panel, he was inducted into the Baseball Hall of Fame. It was hard for him to believe it all started right here fifty summers ago. Never in a million years did he think visiting his grandpa that summer would shape the rest of his life, and baseball for that matter. And in a quiet moment of introspection he thought about his grandpa, his memoir, and how it influenced him to latch onto the game of baseball and never let go.

He stood up from the bench and walked to the lake's edge to take one last look.

"That was one helluva speech you gave today, kid," a voice from behind said.

David's eyes opened wide. He knew the voice. He could never forget it.

"I can still call you *kid* can't I?"

"Arthur?" David asked keeping his gaze glued to the lake. "Were you there?"

"You think I'd miss that?"

David turned and Arthur stood with his hands resting on the back of the bench. He was wearing his newsboy hat and looked exactly the same. He hadn't aged a day. Why would he? Arthur looked at David like a proud father.

"They were all so proud of you today," Arthur said.

"They were there, too?"

"Damn right they were. And Christy says he wants his little notebook back. He thinks it'll be worth something now that you're in the Hall of Fame," Arthur said laughing.

"Tell him *no way*. I've got more notes to take; more sto-ries to write."

They paused for a moment and the wind picked up, ruf-fling the trees.

"What about my grandfather? Does he know?"

"Of course he does. He was there, too. He's so proud. Thrilled beyond words."

Up until this point, David kept his emotions in check. He thought all week he would shed tears during his speech, but somehow he held it in. The mention of his grandfather coming from the mouth of Arthur Page was all he could take and he began to cry. Arthur watched, giving him his space.

"I think about him often," David said.

"He knows that," Arthur reassured him.

David leaned down and picked up a smooth rock and threw it into the still water.

"By the way, you know it's real don't you?"

"Real?"

"The called shot ball."

"I never doubted it for a second. I just hope he was fulfilled when he found out."

"Beyond! It was a tremendous load of his shoulders. By the way, thank you for all of your help with that."

David glanced at his watch.

"You better get going. Your family's waiting." Arthur said.

"I know."

They held their gaze on one another when Arthur extended his hand. David latched onto it and they shook hands for the first time.

"Congratulations, David. You've been an extraordinary asset to this game."

"Thank you."

David started to walk back.

"Oh David…"

He stopped.

"You realize your credentials give you complete access to the Hall *and* the vault. If you ever want to see your grandpa and the others."

"But he never played. What jersey would I put on?"

"As long as it's flannel it doesn't matter."

Arthur winked and walked to his battered row boat. He untied the rope, let it fall into the water, and shoved the boat away from the shore. The boat began to drift away and David noticed the word HEREAFTER scrawled across the back in faded white paint. It made him smile, inside and out.

"See you later, David," Arthur said.

"But when?"

"It all depends."

Arthur waved and dipped his oars into the water.

David watched Arthur row his boat into the open lake and beyond. It had been fifty years since he met Christy, Ty, Walter and Honus; fifty years since he came face to face with baseball's Almighty. With the exception of his Grandfather he never told a soul about that magical summer, not even his wife. And for whatever years he had remaining, the secret would forever stay tucked away in his little black notebook.

After all, who would believe him anyway?

ABOUT THE AUTHOR

~

MATT DAHLGREN WROTE HIS FIRST book in 2007 entitled, *Rumor In Town*. It stemmed from a promise he made to his late grandfather, Babe Dahlgren, the New York Yankees first baseman who replaced Lou Gehrig. He lives in Irvine, California with his wife and three daughters. He can be followed on Twitter: @mattdahlgren12 or visit him at **www.mattdahlgren.com**

ACKNOWLEDGMENTS

A SPECIAL THANK YOU TO Jessica Dahlgren for her wonderful cover painting – it's just how I envisioned it; Jason Sitzes for his editing; Rita Milhollin for encouraging me; Scott Strosnider, Jim Hart, Matt Lovenduski, John Dal Poggetto, Glenn Christy, Greg Chang, Andy Fox and Jeff Staudt for their enduring friendship; Rita Rizor for her unwavering courage. Thank you to John, Aimee and Pete for what is an unbreakable bond. Their support is always felt. An unending thank you to my dear Mom and Dad who make each day better just knowing they're in it. Thank you to my sweet girls Abby, Emma and Penny for the stories you tell me when you don't even realize you're telling them – I write for you and always will. And to my loving wife, Jenny, a thank you seems trivial. She heard this story when it was just a thought, put up with my mood swings while I wrote it and made sure I crossed the finish line. Her radiant smile inspires me throughout each and every day. Finally and most importantly, I want to thank God.

Made in the USA
Charleston, SC
13 September 2015